Praise fo

"A blend of SF and martial arts with a strong element of fantasy . . . there's plenty of fighting, to keep the plot moving. Entertaining."
—*Science Fiction Chronicle*

"[An] auspicious debut . . . a good, solid read."
—Steve Perry

"The action is nonstop and deadly, the details compelling, the story surefooted and satisfying."
—Rutledge Etheridge, author of *The First Duelist*

Laicy Campbell came to Earth to learn the way of the sword . . . and the way of the Zen masters.

But it was on the planet Rune, in the brutal deserts that she at last discovered the task she was meant for, the temple that must be rebuilt. And the shadow warrior who would lead her to her ultimate destination as a searcher and a samurai. She would be called IROSHI . . .

Now Iroshi returns in Cary Osborne's riveting new novel . . .

THE GLAIVE

THE GLAIVE

CARY OSBORNE

ACE BOOKS, NEW YORK

This book is an Ace original edition,
and has never been previously published.

THE GLAIVE

An Ace Book / published by arrangement with the author

PRINTING HISTORY
Ace edition / May 1996

All rights reserved.
Copyright © 1996 by Cary Osborne.
Cover art by Jean-François Podevin.
This book may not be reproduced in whole or in part,
by mimeograph or any other means, without permission.
For information address: The Berkley Publishing Group,
200 Madison Avenue, New York, NY 10016.

The Putnam Berkley World Wide Web site address is
http://www.berkley.com

ISBN: 0-441-00328-1

ACE®
Ace Books are published by The Berkley Publishing Group,
200 Madison Avenue, New York, NY 10016.
ACE and the "A" design are trademarks
belonging to Charter Communications, Inc.

PRINTED IN THE UNITED STATES OF AMERICA

10 9 8 7 6 5 4 3 2 1

1

A sob broke from Iroshi. Tears streamed down her cheeks. The pain was almost more than she could bear.

On a distant world, Lucas was dying. A former lover and teacher, a constant friend, his life ebbed in her service, in the service of the Glaive.

"Don't mourn so, Iroshi," he said. "I will always be with you and the others."

"I know," she replied. "But you shouldn't be suffering so. And it will never be the same."

Pain surged through his body. She felt every nuance almost as intensely as he did. When the spasm subsided, he spoke again.

"It will be better in some ways. I'll be able to concentrate on whatever matter is at hand without my body's needs interfering. I can be with you at a moment's . . . "

A sinking sensation took his breath away. Blackness surged from all sides.

"I must get ready," he said.

"I know. Goodbye, my friend."

His thoughts turned inward. Janue quit relaying and began coaxing. Iroshi backed away. She opened her eyes, tears blurring her vision of the meditation chamber. In a few moments, the Lucas she had known would be gone. He would enter revay, become a loose spirit, and soon after take his place as one of the companions. It was possible that he would live forever.

Yet, she would miss his physical presence. His constant support. Once he was bonded to a host, her contact with him would be direct, although rare.

Reports came in from others, both companions and hosts, on what had happened. Ensi accumulated them, sifting through for pertinent details to report to her later, waiting out of respect for her grief.

Lucas was not the first of the hosts to die since the Guild of the Glaive had come into existence twenty-three years earlier, but none had been murdered before. Lucas was the first with that dubious honor, and the reasons were of paramount importance.

On the rare occasions of death, Iroshi, as head of the Glaive, experienced each member's dying, soothing or coaxing as necessary. However, Lucas's death was especially painful. They had known each other a very long time, since before the Glaive, even before Iroshi. She was Laicy Campbell when they met, a ronin, wandering the known worlds, a warrior without a war or someone to fight for. She had worked hard to establish a reputation as a warrior and, sometimes, a troublemaker. Lucas had given her the name "Iroshi" in those days. It had meant "woman warrior" once, in some long-dead alien language he had learned.

She shook her head. No time to reminisce. Time to get to work, figure out what happened and prevent anything like it from happening again.

"Ensi?"

Yes, her companion answered.

"Are you ready?"

Yes, I have the data condensed and at hand.

He always knew what she needed and, most often, the moment she needed it. They had, after all, shared the same body for all of those twenty-three years.

"Show me," Iroshi said.

She settled back into the round chaise and closed her eyes while the events unrolled in her mind.

It was dark, late night, and Lucas walked along a narrow alley alone. His mind was troubled: the negotiations for the marriage had not gone well that day—a most frustrating occurrence, especially since the preceding seven days had not gone well, either.

Worst thing was, neither he nor Janue could come up with the exact reason, thus preventing a solution. Their eavesdropping was limited by the rules as always, but normally, when major obstacles stood in the way of what everyone seemed to want, those obstacles were foremost in the minds of the participants and were easy to read without probing.

Not this time. These people simply did not know how to negotiate; or their methods were alien to him. And because of the delays, his temper was beginning to get out of hand. But, as a truthsayer, he was expected to remain calm, calming others usually just with this presence.

He could only hope that he did not get any more dynastic marriages for a while. Give him a business contract any time. They were so much less emotional.

Lucas, be aware, Janue, his companion, warned suddenly.

"What is it?"

Lucas placed his hand on the hilt of his sword.

Several men coming this way. They seem in an ugly mood. Shall I probe for the cause?

He knew well that probing people's minds, except in cases of great danger, was forbidden within the guild. The ugly mood must be more than that simple statement made it out to be.

"Yes, if you think it necessary."

Janue's presence disappeared a moment as it always did when he concentrated on others. Lucas had never quite gotten used to the feeling of loss. It had been easier to grow accustomed to the feeling of the companion's presence in his mind when they were first bonded.

They are looking for you. There are seven . . . no, eight of them. Too many for us to fight off.

"Why are they looking for me?"

He drew his sword and looked for a doorway or somewhere to hide discreetly.

Anger. Anger at the interference of the Glaive in the affairs of their world.

"Which world?"

He could hear footsteps and voices around the next corner. He turned to retrace his steps. Nowhere to hide—get some distance between them and him instead.

Here—Bosque. I get an impression of an organization dedicated to fighting the Glaive. Something we have not heard of before.

Another group is ahead. Smaller. They intend to cut you off. They knew where to find you.

He had gotten lazy. Instead of varying his path back to the palace complex, he had taken the quickest way. Too many times. Become predictable and risk your life.

Lights danced into view in front and behind, each followed by a crowd of men with power torches. Lucas pressed his back against the stone wall surrounding someone's garden. The sweet smell of flowers wafted over the wall. Moving toward him were thirteen men. Almost half of them had guns.

It had been five years since he had needed a weapon. These days, the sword was carried more as part of the uniform of a member of the Guild of the Glaive. Even so, he was still quite able to use it to good effect. Except against half a dozen laser pistols.

"I don't know what you men want, but . . ."

"We want you off our world," someone shouted in a Galician accent.

They were operating like a mob, but even he could sense organization at work here.

"I was invited . . ." he said, trying again. They shouted him down.

"Leave our affairs to us."

"We don't need the damn Glaive's interference."

A pistol fired. Janue shouted a warning. He jumped to the right, and the beam passed near but harmlessly. Lucas sprang at the nearest man holding a gun. With a quick swipe of the sword, he knocked the gun to the pavement. Bringing the blade back around, he sliced the next man's upper arm. The man's scream rose above the general clamor.

Lucas pushed him aside, threatened another man with the sword point, and he backed away. Just as he pushed a fourth man, Janue shouted another warning. A searing pain caught him in the back. Janue's gasp echoed his own. The smell of burnt flesh momentarily chafed his throat.

He tried to wheel on the assailant, but his knees buckled and he went down. A second pain caught him in the left side, bending him over. His forehead touched the cool pavement. For a moment that was all he was conscious of. Then cheers filled the air above him. That stopped abruptly when a siren sounded, distant but closing fast.

That was the last Lucas knew until he awoke in the hospital. While he lay unconscious, Janue had contacted Iroshi, whose first thought was to send her own medical team since Galicia's was not so sophisticated. However, there was no way to get them there in time. One of his lungs was gone and his liver was irreparably damaged.

Not enough time.

The images faded, then disappeared altogether. Now they must rush to get two Glaive members to Galicia: one a novice to act as host to Lucas and the other to temporarily host Janue. This was a critical time for Lucas because he must be prepared to leave his body, to enter revay for the first time. It was also the first time he would experience the multiple contacts that only the companions knew. Possibly more traumatic would be the severing of the connection between Lucas and Janue.

This separation had been described as every bit as painful as an amputation without anesthetic by the few who had experienced it.

"All right, Ensi," Iroshi said. "What do we know about the men who killed him?"

She rubbed her hands together to stop their trembling. Experiencing the shooting had been more difficult than she had imagined. Get to work—shake off the effects.

It is possible they were all members of this new organization. One that we have not heard of before. They seem to be afraid of the Glaive's intentions. The impression is that they believe we intend to take control of all governments and corporations.

"You don't sound convinced."

Their anger is strong enough to be real. However, I feel something else, something behind this obvious reaction. It is not clear. Perhaps I imagine it.

"Don't dismiss that feeling too soon. Keep looking into it. Meanwhile, can we identify the men who were actually there?"

Yes, or some of them.

"We'll track them down so they can be questioned."

What if the police of Galicia or Bosque get to them first?

Iroshi shrugged. "It would save us some time. I rather doubt that they will get them all. And the police don't have our means of gathering information."

She considered a moment.

"I'll go on ahead and make arrangements for Lucas's body." She squeezed her eyelids shut, trying to hold back sudden tears. "I wish I could talk to him. Be sure that he's all right."

He is all right, Iroshi, Ensi assured her. A trace of disapproval edged his words, but he did not remind her that she should stay on Rune-Nevas. *Janue will keep me posted. You know that Lucas must concentrate on what she teaches him at this time.*

"Yes, I know. But . . ."

This was the first time she had lost an old friend within the Glaive. The feeling of helplessness was difficult to bear.

"Anyway," she continued, "make arrangements to send the next candidates to Galicia. We have a truthsayer candidate ready, don't we?"

Yes. There will be a truthsayer for Lucas. But only one novice is ready. We will have to send an established member for Janue. She can lie dormant until her host is ready.

"Good." Iroshi brushed a hand across her eyes. She was tired, and the ache in her heart was just beginning. "I'm going to rest now. Let me know when Ferguson has the racer ready."

Ensi withdrew, leaving her to memories and sorrow. And wondering. Was experiencing Lucas's death the worst part of the whole ordeal? Or might it be seeing his body consumed by fire?

It was decided in the early days of the Glaive that when hosts died, their bodies would be cremated. This removed any false hope that some might have of returning to their own bodies, to the lives best left behind. So far, it had made the transition from host to companion less traumatic. However, the day might come when that decision would have to be reversed.

Not today, thank goodness. That was one problem that could be avoided until medical science complicated matters again.

Iroshi pushed to the edge of the chaise and stood up. Her body felt old, more than its forty-eight years. As she left the meditation chamber, she wondered when Ensi would chastise her for endangering herself by going to Bosque.

Later that night, as they got ready for bed, it was Mitchell who argued against her going.

"You shouldn't endanger yourself," he said. "If Lucas wasn't prepared, what makes you think you will be?" He stretched out on the bed.

She had told him the whole story of Lucas's death at the hands of a mob and what the reason appeared to be.

"I know there is danger. The attack on Lucas . . ."

". . . could be repeated when you get there." He sighed, and she lay down beside him and put her arm over him. "At least take extra precautions," he went on. "Take guns and not just your swords. And I want you to take a couple of bodyguards. At least."

"I will," she said as she brushed his lips with her fingertips. "Don't worry. We'll be careful."

He turned toward her, put his arms around her, and pulled her to him.

"You better," he said. "I'll never forgive you if you get yourself killed. No one else would keep me in this job."

She chuckled. That morning he had complained about

how much work administering the Glaive had become. Not like the old days when assignments had been fewer and most of them a lot closer to home. She did worry a little sometimes about his workload. Thank goodness another governor of Rune-Nevas had been elected and he no longer had that additional responsibility.

She kissed him, love washing through her body and mind as strongly as it ever had. It was wonderful knowing that he was always there for her to come home to.

2

✦

Black smoke rose into the still air. Sweat ran down the small of her back. They were the only two things Iroshi had noticed for more than two hours. Those around her—officials from Galicia—stirred restlessly. They wanted to get inside where it was cooler, but clearly felt they could not leave the platform until the chief mourner went in.

Iroshi wanted to stay until the last ember went out but, even under the awning, the heat of the sun and from the funeral pyre made her lightheaded. Fainting would not make a positive impression.

We had better go inside, Ensi said gently. *Nothing more can be accomplished here.*

"He was my friend."

I know.

She sighed, fighting back tears.

He is still with us.

"I will never hear his voice, his laughter, or feel his touch." She swallowed another sigh. "He is not with us until I can talk to him."

Soon.

Iroshi nodded her head and turned toward her hosts.

"Shall we go inside?" Tarek Varia asked. Her face

was flushed under the tall purple fez that was a symbol of her office. Even the lightweight, blue gown showed dark perspiration wetness in places where the cloth touched her body. Iroshi's own grey dress uniform probably didn't look much better.

She nodded again and Varia, the chief councilor of Galicia, led the way. As they stepped down, the Greer brothers, Erik, and Mark, two warriors of the Glaive, fell in step behind. Mitchell had insisted the two weight lifters come with her, and this time she had not protested.

After one last look back, she let herself be led away, the group following inside, a look of relief on most faces. Varia gave orders to her staff to bring refreshments into the meeting room. A large oval table sat in the middle, surrounded by padded leather chairs. After the bright heat, the room was cool, almost dark with its indirect lighting.

Everyone spoke in hushed voices as they milled around the table, waiting for her to take her seat on one side.

Gods!

Gripping the back of the chair, Iroshi tried to push down the anger that had nearly consumed her since her arrival. They were all so impotent. . . . So far, no progress had been made in finding Lucas's killers, and every government representative seemed totally unable to decide on a course of action. As far as she could tell, they had spent the seven days since the attack arguing over who should be in charge of the investigation.

Servants came in and loudly placed trays of finger

foods and pitchers of cold drink at various places around the table. One of each was set within reach of her chair. Iroshi sat down, and the servant ceased hovering and poured a glass of cold tea. Usually she preferred hot tea, but after the heat outside, a cold beverage was more suitable.

She picked up the cloth napkin and dabbed first at her mouth, then at the rest of her face. Both the tea and the climate control in the room were beginning to make her feel cooler. She sat back and closed her eyes a moment, concentrating on thoughts of ice and winter nights on Rune-Nevas.

"We may begin," Varia said from across the table.

Chairs creaked softly as they took weight. Talking dropped to a murmur, then stopped altogether. Iroshi opened her eyes and bowed slightly toward her host, who smiled.

"First," Varia said, "I want to welcome you, Iroshi, to our world and I hope that, in spite of the reason for your coming here, your stay will be as pleasant as possible. Second, let me say how saddened all of us are that a member of the Guild of the Glaive met his death in Galicia. Let me assure you, everything will be done—is being done—to solve this crime."

She stopped and indicated another councilor with her hand. The man rose and began expressing his condolences and welcome. When he finished, the next councilor, a woman, rose to do the same, and Iroshi realized they all intended to speak. A quick count confirmed there were fourteen, including the chief councilor.

"Ensi, can we interrupt this without causing too much of a fuss?"

If you do not, we could be here until well after nightfall, he replied, clearly put out by the waste of time. *However,* he continued, *long speeches and drawn-out ceremonies are their normal way of proceeding.*

"Presumably one reason Lucas was unable to get any agreement on the marriage. Thank goodness no one from Aulda or the Bosque council is here."

The fourth speaker stood, and Iroshi smiled at him.

"We can use the time to get better acquainted with the councilors, then," she continued silently.

Had he been able, he would have frowned. For several reasons, he disliked getting into other people's minds and heartily approved of the restrictions placed on scanning. Thankfully, he was rarely detected, unlike the first time he had approached her in the temple ruin on Rune-Nevas. That time he had entered for different reasons and had intended that she be conscious of his presence.

I will be careful, he said and drifted away.

As far as Lucas had been able to determine, the people of Galicia—the whole continent, not just the capital city—had no extrasensory abilities. This should give Ensi the opportunity to delve more deeply than he would if the opposite were true. Of the people of Aulda, little was known as yet.

Varia sat with a smile on her pretty face while half of the councilors said their little rehearsed speeches. Iroshi acknowledged each in turn, hoping her attitude indicated appreciation for their words. With Ensi gone, thoughts of Lucas crowded in. For all their words, these people had no idea who Lucas was—they saw him as a truth-sayer, a warrior of the Glaive, whom they had invited to arbitrate a dynastic marriage.

She remembered a loving man who had taught her much about being a warrior and about being a woman. They were lovers only a short time; she was always on the move in those days. But, when she was ready to establish the Guild of the Glaive, he was one of the first she had sought out. It had taken a while, but finding him had been worth the effort. Within the Glaive, he had been her right-hand man, her confidant, and had accepted that they could not be lovers again.

That was because of Mitchell. Constable Mitchell. Former Governor Mitchell. Her anchor, the man she loved most in life, who never fully understood the members of the Glaive but worked for years as their administrator. He had no extrasensory abilities either, could never be a full member, but without him, the Glaive would not have achieved as much as it had.

He was also the one person who had foreseen most clearly the possibility that resentment would rise. He had voiced his opinion several times and, because of his cautionary words, they had often moved more slowly than even their limited numbers required. Still, in spite of all their precautions, it had happened. Or, so it would seem from events here on Bosque.

With a start, Iroshi realized the last councilor had made his speech and sat back down. She cleared her throat and stood.

"I thank you all for your kind expressions of sympathy," she said. "I know from his reports that Lucas took his assignment here very seriously. However, at the same time, he enjoyed visiting your world and your people. He wanted very much to be of help in the negotiations.

"I and the other members of the Glaive want the people of Galicia to know that we do not hold their government responsible for the murder of our friend. And we appreciate all of your efforts at bringing the murderers to justice."

She sat back down as the councilors all nodded knowingly. It was late, probably dark outside. No more would be accomplished until tomorrow. Varia rose and said as much.

"We will meet again tomorrow," the chief councilor continued, "if that is agreeable with you." Iroshi nodded. "Police reports on actions taken thus far will be presented, and any suggestions you might be able to make . . ." She spread her hands wide to include everyone at the table.

"We are adjourned until tomorrow morning, then."

All of the councilors stood, the rustle of their robes whispering around the room. Each one came up to Iroshi and shook hands with her, something they had done when she first arrived. Goodnights said, she walked back outside. The night was nearly as hot as the day had been. In spite of the thick forests covering much of the world, the climate seemed more like a desert.

Erik and Mark fell in behind. Capital guards, who had been assigned to her during her stay, surrounded the three of them. Clearly, the councilors were intent on making sure nothing else befell a member of the Glaive during this visit.

Backlit by twenty-foot pole lamps, smoke from the pyre still rose into the air. Because of the intense flames from gas jets placed under the pyre, only glowing ash remained on the funerary dais. Once cooled, the ashes would be gathered up for transport back to Rune-Nevas, where they would be scattered in the desert. She looked away, concentrating instead on the guest wing across the compound.

The stucco-white walls of the buildings reflected the shifting, red glow. The square outlines stood out against the whiter background of the city lights, quiet now in the night. They had the entire east wing, a suite of rooms that would more than house her party. Of course, when the rest arrived the extra rooms would be filled.

Mark preceded her into the suite while she and Erik stood just inside the doorway. The great room was large and simply furnished; few hiding places there. Mark disappeared into the group of four bedrooms to the right, and she moved into the center of the room. Physically checking every corner and closet took longer than the companions' telepathic search, but they were taking no chances.

She took the time to survey her surroundings. White, beige, and teal were the dominant colors. Two sofas facing each other. Six chairs—large, overstuffed style—sat about the great room. Appropriate number of tables. A bar close to the right wall. Comfortable enough.

Mark passed through the great room, then disappeared again, this time into the master bedroom, two other bed-

rooms and a utility room to the left. Another few moments and he gave the all-clear through Ensi. Coming
back into the great room, he took a chair near the door,
while Erik said goodnight and went to his room next to
hers. Meanwhile, Ensi confirmed that the capital guards
had taken their places outside the door and around the
outside of the wing.

A pitcher of tea and glasses waited on the bar. She
emptied it into the sink and brewed another pot. When it
was done, she poured herself a glass and offered one to
Mark. He accepted it, then returned to the chair in the
corner of the living room. His relaxed posture belied the
alertness of his mind and that of his companion. It also
masked the tension he felt. All of them were tense and
expectant of trouble of some kind, but the brothers were
warriors, pure and simple, and utterly devoted to her.

She carried her own glass into the bedroom and un-
slung the sword and scabbard from her back. She took
off the jacket of her uniform and her boots and sat on the
edge of the bed. Gods! She was tired but too keyed up to
sleep. In fact, there had not been a good night's sleep
since Lucas's death.

Maids or servants had unpacked her bags and very
carefully placed the shinai and wakizashi on the dresser.
After a moment's debate, she chose the bamboo shinai.
The room was big enough so that using the shorter
sword was not necessary.

Only the motions of practice. The void eluded her,
taunted her with its promise of forgetfulness and peace.
She would not be one with the surroundings tonight.
Everything reminded her of Lucas—all of the times they

had practiced together and consulted together on one problem or another.

How must Janue be feeling? She had been closer to him than anyone.

She froze in mid-stride. Janue. Yes, the effect on her must be traumatic indeed. Something she had not fully considered before. What would be the long-term effect on the companions of losing one host after another? The companions were ageless. Unfortunately, the hosts were not. A hundred and twenty years might be the expected life span of the living bodies; ninety or a hundred of those years in which the body and mind were shared. That was a very long relationship and, although its end must be anticipated, the reality of it must be almost paralyzing. Would the members hold up under the strain?

"Ensi."

Yes.

"You and I melded long before any of the other members. How will it be for us when I die?"

A long pause before the answer came.

It will be nearly as difficult as our entering revay all those years ago when the temple was overrun. I was selected to contact you because we were most alike. It is difficult to imagine finding anyone else with whom I would be as comfortable.

"That problem has just occurred to me again, as it relates to all members. In the rare instances when it has been necessary, we have paired up host and companion as each was available. Except in the early days, little thought has been given to compatibility."

Mitchell has wondered about it.

"He's never said anything."

*I would guess that is because he feels that he under-
stands us too little.*

"We'll have to discuss this when we get back. We
must make sure the pairings are appropriately done. And
we will have to study the possible problems suffered by
both companion and host on the death of the host."

Ensi shrugged mentally.

*So far, our selection criteria have worked very well.
But you are right: this is something we have not given
enough thought to.*

That settled for the time being, practice continued.
The movements became more natural, smoother, although she still could not enter the void. The loss of self,
of being one with her surroundings, did not always happen.

At last, her body said enough. She put the shinai back
on the dresser and got a towel from the bathroom. Void
or not, she had worked up a sweat. Sleep would probably come more easily now. Especially after a long
shower.

She had just unbuttoned her shirt when someone
knocked on the door of the suite.

Mark was ready, Ensie told her, meaning that he had
known someone was at the door before the knock came.
Erik is alerted.

"Who is it?" she asked Ensi.

*His name is Jiron Yail, a local policeman. He is un-
armed.*

"I guess we had better let him in. Tell Mark."

She rebuttoned her shirt and put on her boots, all the

while listening. Mark opened the door. The visitor introduced himself, then Mark came to get her.

"Impression?" she asked him.

"He seems tense. Looks like he has something on his mind."

She nodded, put on her jacket, and went out to meet the visitor. Yail, dressed in the blue and gold uniform of the Capital City police, looked to be around twenty-five. His brown eyes appraised her with a directness that she instantly liked. From the look on his face, he *was* on a very serious errand. He introduced himself, and she offered him a seat.

Iroshi assumed a relaxed pose on the sofa, her feet tucked under her as she leaned against the arm. Behind her, Mark had resumed his chair in the corner. Yail sat stiffly on the facing sofa, clearly considering how to begin.

"Does coming here endanger your life?" Iroshi asked.

Yail looked up from contemplating his hands lying in his lap. He reached up to push back a lock of dark blond hair that had strayed to his forehead.

"I heard you were an astute observer," he said. "Yes, there could be problems, at least with my career. I'm going over my superiors' heads."

"What excuse did you give the guards?"

He blushed.

"Something they had no reason to doubt."

She nodded and waited for him to continue.

"The real reason I came is that I was assigned to this case of yours. You've probably guessed by now that the police have done very little to find your man's killer. It's doubtful that anything positive will be achieved."

He pushed at the lock of hair again. Iroshi and Ensi realized simultaneously that the apprehension he displayed came as much from excitement as from fear. The kind of excitement that he often found in his profession, and that he tended to savor like some men savor a passionate embrace. He also expected his handsome appearance to work its charm on her. He relied on his looks to have a positive effect, a trait that she did not need Ensi to discover for her.

"There is a conspiracy on the part of the Council to restrict the police in this matter," he said. "Not so much against the Glaive. It seems to be out of fear of this new group that has sprung up."

"Do you know what this group calls itself?" she asked.

"No. I don't think it has a name as yet. At least, not one that's gotten around."

"But it's the group that is supposed to be fighting the influence of the Glaive."

"Yes. It is very new, but reports say its numbers are growing rapidly here on Bosque. It's the fact of its growing numbers that seems to have officials taking the group into account. That, and the fact that some of the members come from several powerful families."

"You come from a powerful family of Galicia yourself, don't you?" Iroshi asked. Another fact that Ensi had ferreted out.

He looked startled by the question, but recovered his equilibrium quickly.

"They have some influence, yes. But their influence does not go beyond. Not even across the ocean to Aulda."

"Still, your family must have some feelings regarding the presence of the Glaive. Do they resent us?"

He thought a moment. Iroshi got up, poured herself some tea, and offered him some. He shook his head.

She walked back toward the sofa.

"I can't speak for everyone in my family—we number almost two hundred. However, I think it would be safe to say that the majority appreciates the assistance the Glaive has consented to give our world on this occasion. Closer relations with Aulda will benefit nearly every business in Galicia. After all, we are the two major political and economic powers on Bosque."

She sat down, turned from contemplating the brown liquid in the glass to the liquid brown of Yail's eyes.

"They thought that Lucas's efforts were meeting with some success, then?"

"They . . . Why are you asking about my family? We have no association with the anti-Glaive group. We are a business family for the most part. A few others have outside dealings, but I am the only one who has not taken any part in the operation of the corporation."

"However true that may be, your family must be representative of certain feelings here in Galicia. At least to a point. I suppose . . ."

He is not wishing to hide anything. He is, however, a private man in spite of the manner in which he uses his physical appearance to gain confidence.

"No harm in using all of one's assets," Iroshi commented silently.

"I meant no offense," she continued aloud. "Now, do you have any details on the efforts to keep the police from finding Lucas's killers?"

For the next few minutes, Yail described anonymous communications that had been received by members of the Council and certain police officials for several weeks. Most of them had described dire consequences of various kinds that would follow if the Glaive was allowed to continue influencing politics and important decisions—either dynastic or business—on the populated worlds. The hints of terrible things that might befall officials if they did not heed the warnings could be frightening for a lot of people.

"Tarek Varia is not an especially brave woman," he said. "Politically, she tends to step back and let conflicting forces take each other out. That keeps her from having to make really hard decisions."

He said nothing of how he knew the contents of these communications or to whom they had been addressed. Admitting that he had broken into offices or gotten a couple of young women to do it for him was not in his plans.

"Events may quite likely overcome her one day," Iroshi said.

Yail nodded agreement.

"It does seem strange that such a movement would spring up here on Bosque, considering that this is our first venture here," she went on almost to herself. "I would suspect their leader is a visitor."

She paused as if contemplating the ramifications of that fact, all the while feeling his gaze. She looked up suddenly, their eyes met, and he looked away after several seconds.

"Why did you decide to take a chance by coming to me?"

"I am a policeman," he answered with no sign of having lost his composure. "I believe in what I do. Most of my superiors feel the same way, but their hands are tied more securely than mine."

"Are you freer to act because of your family?"

"That, and sometimes being lower echelon is an advantage. I am less visible and less likely to be watched."

"What excuse did you use to get in here? Just in case something is said tomorrow."

He grinned self-consciously. "I told the guards you had slipped me a note asking me to meet you here."

"For personal rather than professional reasons?"

He nodded. There was the sense that romantic liaisons of this sort were not uncommon on Galicia. That the grin was self-conscious *did* indicate, however, that Yail realized that it might not be common practice where Iroshi came from.

He had expected her to be angry, maybe even embarrassed. Her lack of reaction clearly puzzled him, but he covered this very well, too. He would probably be disappointed if she confessed that she did not remember him at all among the events of the day. However, there were more important matters to get back to.

"Since the police are officially doing little to find the

killers," she began, "have *you* come across any clues to their identities?"

It was easy to believe that Yail had been doing his own investigating.

"I am sure that I have identified at least two of the men: one an off-worlder and the other from here. As you said, the organizers would most likely be from someplace other than Galicia, and that was where I looked."

"Why did you reach that conclusion?"

"It's not the sort of movement that would begin here on its own. We're an aggressive people in business; we tend to pursue those goals overtly. In negotiations, we are condescending, even self-effacing. Then too, there have been numerous reports of similar organizations elsewhere, although this seems to be the most overt incident so far."

"You keep yourself well informed," she said.

He beamed at the compliment that he had at last garnered.

"Can you keep me informed of your progress as long as I am here?" she continued.

"Of course. How long do you plan to stay?"

"I'm not quite sure. I want to begin my own investigation; I'm sure that is expected. Another Glaive racer should arrive in two days for more private ceremonies relating to Lucas's death and cremation." She looked at the clock on the wall.

"Now, I would suggest that we have spent enough time together for a first night. Should I tell the guards that you will be returning?"

"No. It is expected."

"Goodnight, then."

Iroshi stood, shook hands with the young policeman, and saw him out. Mark smiled a moment as she turned back into the room—a clear sign that, in spite of her being bonded to Mitchell *pro tempore* for over twenty years, tales of her earlier sexual escapades still colored her reputation. She fully expected one day to come across some epic poem recounting them. And more that had never occurred.

As head of the Guild of the Glaive, everything about her had become larger than life. It was an image she had fostered even before creating the Glaive, and something she was now forced to live with.

Thoughts of Mitchell brought a touch of homesickness; she always missed him a great deal.

"Any further impressions, Ensi?" she asked, pushing other thoughts aside as she walked back toward the bedroom.

Yes. Although he does not seem aware of it, Yail may have some extrasensory abilities, the first we have found here. He seems to maintain a vague barrier against contact. Probing his thoughts and feelings is not difficult, but any contact should be made very carefully. His vanity over his appeal to women is extravagant but makes him no less personable.

"I knew that," she interrupted.

There is a rift between him and his family, Ensi continued without noticing. *Probably over his not going into the business. The young man craves adventure.*

"All of which we can make use of in one way or another."

Will you . . .

"He is too young," she interrupted again.

But you are attracted to him.

"In a remote sort of way."

In spite of their long-term relationship, she and Mitchell had never made a vow of fidelity. Brief interludes had occurred for both of them, but not in a long time. Maybe they were getting too old.

"Was Yail attracted to me?"

You could not tell?

"Never mind."

I will never understand women.

"That's the first sexist remark you've made in years, Ensi. And it's not true. You understand me all too well."

I know, he almost sighed. *Ours is a more intimate experience than physical coupling ever was. More satisfying in some ways to feel passion in both parties.*

They both knew he was being facetious; he always slipped away during her sexual encounters.

Back in the bedroom she stripped off her uniform and picked up the shinai. Although she had practiced enough before, this was the best way to bring this discussion to a close. Or to keep from calling Yail back.

After the first few moments, the old man appeared from her thoughts and they fought, his traditional kendo moves matching her own. They had fought many times since that first night in the temple ruins on Rune-Nevas. His shadow glided along the wall, the two bamboo swords smashing against each other, the sound only in her mind.

Very rarely did she take a spar along these days. The

original mechanical practice device had given out years
ago and, even though the newer ones had many more
features, she found them less satisfying. Perhaps they
were too perfect, never actually harming their human ad-
versaries like the old ones could. A few small scars
marked her body and limbs as proof of occasional care-
lessness. Still, she needed to keep up with the gadgets
and accessories her people used. Sort of like listening to
the younger ones' music in order to understand what
they talked about.

After half an hour, she stopped. Still too much on her
mind to even approach the void, but she had worked up
a sweat again. She put away the shinai, stepped into the
bathroom, and stripped off her underwear. Her naked reflection stared back from the mirrored wall. The pale
skin, glistening with sweat, was stretched tightly over a
slender body. Not too slender, but not the more rounded
figure that was the current fashion, either. Not bad for
her age.

Every decade she said the same thing. She turned and
studied the back view. A couple of tucks had kept the
breasts and buttocks from sagging. Vanity, thy name is
Iroshi, to paraphrase.

Had Yail been attracted to her? Or was his body language and eye contact a result of much practice?

She dismissed the reflection with a wave, turned her
back on it, and stepped into the shower. As hot water,
then cold water, washed over her, she and Ensi discussed how to proceed. So far, by examining Janue's
memories, he had tentatively identified two of the con-
spirators. Might they be the same ones Yail thought he

had identified? Although personal vengeance demanded they all be punished, the most important task was to trace the origins of the as yet unnamed group that opposed the Glaive. How to do that without appearing to fear its influence or actions was an important consideration. They must not lend the organization more credence than it yet deserved.

What was its name? It had to have a name.

Rhea Walker studied the door even though Carson had left ten minutes earlier, closing it behind him and leaving her alone in the dimly lighted room. She had half-expected him to come right back in. The man had no courage. Nor could he see that this action of his had larger consequences than the death of a single man.

She looked away at last, shifting her gaze to the holo cube on the table beside her. Yes, Duncan, it was all coming together. The Glaivers would be on the run soon. The anti-Glaive organization had taken off even better than she had anticipated. And soon the trap would close.

However, Carson might be a hindrance if not an outright danger to everything she had planned. He was still trying too hard to be brave. Once in the hands of the Glaivers, that facade would crumble. It had to. Yes, she could count on him to play his unwitting part.

3

Early morning sunlight streamed through the windows of the meeting room. Dust particles swirled through the light beams in a random dance that mesmerized. They were easier to concentrate on than were the words of the councilors.

Once more Iroshi hammered down frustration and anger that rose in her throat to choke her. Angry words would accomplish nothing, but neither would the aimless babblings of these people

No wonder Lucas had found dealing with them so frustrating. Never before had she encountered people so unwilling to make decisions.

At the moment, they argued again—oh so very politely—over whose jurisdiction the investigation should fall under. It was difficult to tell whether the heads of the law enforcement agencies sought jurisdiction or avoided it. Each professed that he was unworthy to head such an important investigation.

Someone else should have been sent from the Glaive. There were better things to do, and the older she got, the less patience she had.

No. That had never been an option. Not only was Lucas her old and dear friend; everyone, everywhere, had to be shown that killing a member of the Glaive was a serious matter. Her presence demonstrated that. Finding the killers would show that the Glaive was a force to be reckoned with and that it deserved its established reputation.

"Marshal Jeffron. Surely this should have been decided days ago," Varia said.

Her voice was high. Had Madam Chief Councilor become perturbed with them?

"Madam Varia," Marshal Jeffron began.

"Perhaps I can help, Madam Varia," Iroshi interrupted.

Everyone turned to look at the head of the Glaive, their eyebrows raised. She had not spoken at all during the meeting the day before, nor for the past hour and a half this morning. Curiosity was aroused among the majority. Marshal Jeffron leaned back in his chair, arms folded across his chest, staring first at Iroshi, then at Varia.

"I am sure that Marshal Jeffron and all of the law enforcement agents of Galicia have been working very hard in their investigations." Jeffron and Gretzh, his counterpart in the planetary force, looked at each other, then back at her. "However, we of the Glaive have access to other means of investigation. Recently, I was given the names of two men involved in the murder under discussion. One is from the capital and the other is not. Does not your law give jurisdiction to the agency in which the crime was committed? Does it not also dictate jurisdiction to the planetary agency if someone crosses from, let's say, one province to another—or perhaps from a province to the capital city? Would this not mean, then, that both the municipal agency and the planetary agency are involved?"

Varia looked from one man to the other, then nodded agreement. Contact with Yail was already beginning to pay dividends.

"It has never been particularly beneficial to have conflicting jurisdictions," Iroshi continued. "Since the Glaive is the injured party in this case, might we assign jurisdiction?"

Jeffron jumped to his feet.

"Madam Varia, I protest . . ."

"I am so pleased that you wish to volunteer," Iroshi said. "However, because their network is more widespread than the national agency, I was hoping to smooth the way for Commissioner Gretzh's world agency."

That might also free Yail from any official involvement that would make him suspect if he kept seeing the head of the Glaive.

Jeffron collapsed in his seat. Gretzh turned slightly pale. Was he one of those who had received a threat from the assassins? Yail had not mentioned him specifically in that regard.

Gods! Both men were certainly terrified of this case. If their fear was not because of direct threats from the terrorists, had government officials warned them not to work too hard on finding the culprits? Yail's information indicated that might also be the case. Ensi had sensed no direct involvement of any councilor with the terrorists. Perhaps he should also start looking into the more powerful families.

"Excellent idea, Iroshi," Varia said.

The response had certainly taken long enough, but she looked and sounded relieved now that the decision had been taken from in front of her.

"Commissioner Gretzh will lead the investigation. Marshal Jeffron, you will give him all the cooperation he may need."

The faces around the table showed varying emotions, from relief that mirrored Varia's to anger and fear on Gretzh's face.

"Now that that is settled, we have a favor to ask of you, Iroshi," Varia said. "The matter of the marriage between the House of Vargas of Galicia and the House of Walthen of Aulda. Unfortunately, Lucas was taken from us before this was settled. We would like to ask if you would preside over the negotiations."

"Another truthsayer is among those to arrive from the Glaive at midday, Madam Varia. I am sure she would be fully able to take over."

Iroshi, she will be bonding with Lucas. She cannot take on such a task so soon.

"Don't worry, Ensi. I will let myself be persuaded to take over. That will give me a ready excuse for staying in Galicia for a while longer."

You know they hope to gain a semblance of forgiveness by having you take Lucas's place.

"And if we give them that semblance of forgiveness, they might relax a little more. We need for them to be put off guard, even obliged to us, particularly after choosing the World Force to take the case."

"It would mean so much to us if you would take over," Varia was saying.

"Yes, Iroshi," Lindyn Ortega chimed in. She was distantly related to the Vargas family.

"Indeed," someone else spoke up.

"We would be proud."

"Your help would be invaluable."

Feigning reluctance, she gave in. Most faces in the room lit up in gratitude. Jeffron's smile had not faded during the entire discussion.

Once more, the midday sun beat down as Iroshi stood waiting. This time, the wait was for an arrival: the racer bringing Sarah, Lucas's host, and Leila to act as temporary host for Janue. They were accompanied by Sheera and Johnson, who would conduct the ceremony. Lucas's was to be a permanent bonding, the first ever conducted off Rune-Nevas.

The racer landed and taxied to the spot where Iroshi waited. It had taken special permission to avoid the port terminal, but the fewer people involved in the arrival, the better. The hatch opened and the travelers descended, each decked out in uniform except the new host, recognizable by the swath of soft grey hooded cape that hid her from prying eyes.

Protecting her virginity, Iroshi thought wryly. The whole ceremony had become complicated and ritualized and, although she did not like it personally, she recognized the importance within the small community she and others had gathered together. All of those who could not attend physically would join in through the minds of the companions. No one missed a bonding ceremony.

At least the sword-choosing was still private, something she had insisted on in memory of her own choosing at Mushimo's dojo back on Earth. Only she and the new member participated. Although she had never considered it before, it might be possible the choosing would not work with others present.

The relationship between the person and the sword was almost as much a melding as was that between the companion and the host. The spirits of the weapons' owners resided in each weapon. Or, maybe it was only a matter of their influence. Whichever it was, the sword chose the person. She would always believe that.

Anyway, the choosing had to be done on Rune-Nevas, where the collection of weapons was housed in a special room in the Glaive complex. That much would not change as long as she lived.

For years she had scoured the known worlds for swords, pikes, knives—all manner of antique and new-made hand weapons—amassing one of the greatest collections anywhere. The addition of Mushimo's collection had nearly doubled the number of weapons. Wearing a sword was one of the marks of a Glaive member, part of the uniform. Members were allowed to wear them in places where all other weapons were banned.

She and the two brothers stepped forward to embrace the new arrivals. Everyone expressed sadness over the death of one of their own, commiserating with one another as only they could. Yail stood to one side, waiting for them all to pile into the limousine. At Iroshi's request, he had been assigned as her personal liaison as long as she remained in Galicia.

First they went to their quarters in the palace complex to rest and prepare. Late in the evening they took off for the wooded site in the wilderness Iroshi and Ensi had selected the day before. In the midst of old-growth trees, they had sensed that it was an ancient site, although no ruins or signs of habitation remained. In the near-dark, the feeling of lingering spirits was very strong.

Yail helped unload the boxes before he and the driver returned to the city.

"We will be back just after dawn," Yail said. He seemed reluctant to leave.

"Thank you," Iroshi said.

She started away, hesitated, turned toward him, and held out her hand. He took it in his own a moment as their eyes locked on each other. Her pulse beat more rapidly under the pressure of his thumb. Or was it his pulse?

"Tomorrow," she said and hastened away to join the others.

The limousine lifted and sped back toward the city. She turned and watched the air car's lights disappear in the night sky, a feeling of regret seeping into her mind.

"Dirty old woman," she mumbled to herself.

She set to work, helping arrange for the ceremony. Lamps were lit and placed around the circle. Camp chairs were set up for everyone, even Sarah, who had chosen to sit in the center of the circle rather than lie on a mat as some novices preferred. Bonding was an exhausting and often traumatic event no matter how much preparation preceded it. In this case, however, Sarah had been waiting nearly a year for this final step toward membership, and she was eager.

Sheera and Leila took Sarah behind a screen, set her sword aside, and helped her shed the novice's uniform. They then helped her into the long gown. Her new uniform hung in the closet back in Capital City. She would put that on for the first time in private.

"Ensi, check the area, please," Iroshi said as they waited.

He sought outward, joined by the other companions, to ensure no one was within several miles. Meanwhile, Iroshi embraced each of the members present—Sarah last of all—and everyone took a seat.

Facing the new member, Iroshi asked, "Sarah, do you come to this bonding of your own free will?"

"Yes."

"Search your mind, your heart, for any reason you do not want to join with Lucas Kent, spirit companion of the Glaive."

The pause that followed was more for effect than for soul-searching.

"Do you find any reason?"

"No."

"Are there any family members who would block your becoming a member of the Glaive?"

A brother had contacted the Glaive, asking that it deny Sarah membership. The unspoken reason was that he wanted his sister to marry the rich man who had proposed a year earlier, planning to capitalize on the marriage himself. He had no authority to make such a request, since Sarah was of age.

"No."

"Do you wish your bonding to be witnessed by other members of the Glaive?"

"Yes."

Iroshi closed her eyes.

"Then close your eyes and welcome them."

Iroshi caught her breath a moment. It would have been Lucas and Janue as the most senior members who first presented themselves. This time, it was Crowell and Mushimo, her own teachers of years earlier. They greeted Sarah in tandem, as a unit, because it was only through the companions that the hosts could even participate.

They came according to seniority based on the date of bonding. It took a long time, but no one seemed to mind. It was wonderful to "see" friends, some of whom had been gone from Rune-Nevas for years. Afterward, they reflected on their own bondings as they prepared to shed mourning and embrace Lucas in his new existence among them.

The last greeting said, all of them faded into the background except Iroshi and Ensi. She began speaking, both aloud and internally; her voice would guide Sarah and Lucas through this rebirth.

She would miss him so damn much!

Not tonight. What followed was cause for celebration, welcoming, two new beginnings.

"Sarah, relax," Iroshi instructed again. "Look within yourself. Deeper. Deeper. Relax. Deeper."

The girl sank within herself, to the level she had reached before in meditation. Then deeper, guided by Iroshi's voice, until she saw and experienced her own birth. Deeper into Sarah Long than she had ever gone before. In a way, this was the final test. Established members could look one last time for any serious flaw in the novice's character, and she could see if she saw any of the same traits.

"Deeper."

Sarah hesitated. The way led into total darkness, cold, airless. She looked to Iroshi, who nodded. They went on. Once Sarah saw two of her selves merge into one. Images flitted at the edge of seeing. Deeper and deeper. Until she saw him. Lucas, waiting. Lucas, ready to live again through her. Ready to join with her, become her life's companion.

They smiled at one another, and Lucas held out his hand. She went to him. *This* was the moment every novice yearned for, as did every companion without a host. This was what made them members of the Glaive.

"Lucas, Sarah. Are you ready to take the oath?"

"Yes," they both answered.

"Turn and look at each other." They did. For a moment, Iroshi could not take her eyes off Lucas's image: his tall, angular body, strong jaw, twinkling eyes, still-blond hair, and the strong arms that had once embraced her.

"Repeat the oath," she instructed at last.

"I will honor you as a part of me and as a life to yourself," they said. "I will work with you toward achieving the goals of the Glaive. I will protect you from harm. I welcome you into my mind and heart."

Iroshi and Ensi turned from them and began the ascent out of Sarah and Lucas's being. The others followed, quietly.

Iroshi opened her eyes and looked first at Sarah. A smile on the girl's lips, tears streaking her cheeks. It would be a good bonding.

Iroshi.

She jerked awake. A strange voice spoke inside.

It's me, Lucas.

"Lucas. I could hardly wait until I could talk to you." She looked at the clock on the bedside table. Half past one in the morning. "Sarah?"

She's sleeping. She wanted to try on the new uniform so much, but just could not keep her eyes open. I think it will be a good match.

"I am glad. Are you . . . okay?"

He laughed. *Of course. Dying is the worst of it.*

"Soon, Ensi and the others will need your memories of the people who attacked you. We got as much as we could from Janue."

We've already been working on it. Sleep now. I only wanted to let you know I am here. You were so anxious.

"Thank you. And welcome."

He withdrew and she tried to settle back into sleep, but thoughts rambled around in her head. Memories of the ceremony and afterward came unbidden. And not a little guilt.

She had been so glad to see Yail when he stepped out of the limousine. They sat close on the trip back into the city, but fatigue had overpowered any feelings of adventure. Had things been different, she might have invited him to stay the night with her. Dual regrets nagged at her: this was the first time in five or six years she had been tempted to bed someone other than Mitchell, and she had let Yail go back out the door. Her head would be clearer tomorrow night.

Even more exhausted than the rest, Sarah had welcomed help from Sheera in getting into bed. Leila, Janue's temporary host, had been nearly as exhausted. The two young women, inseparable as ever, shared the same dreamless sleep in the same bed. Their joy at Sarah's initiation might be short-lived once they were separated by assignments. A lesson they would have to learn as soon as possible.

Iroshi yawned and turned over on her side. Soon sleep began to settle over her, and memories and thoughts settled back into their niches.

A loud explosion rocked the room. The bed jumped under her. Masonry and bricks rained down on her. She threw her arms over her face, but not in time. Something hit her right temple.

Bright lights sparkled against blackness. Noises, very far away, insisted on attention. Just go back to sleep. Voices, hollering, crying. A scream.

Iroshi sat bolt upright, bumping her head. Dust brought tears to her eyes when she opened them. Which hurt worse? Her head or her eyes?

Shaking her head dislodged dust from her hair. She coughed. Tears streamed down her cheeks, and she opened her eyes a little. Less pain, although she could see little in the dark. A dark form loomed over her. Her raised hands felt a narrow metal beam suspended just above the bed.

The door slammed open and light stabbed into the room. She threw her arm up to shade her eyes.

"Iroshi, are you all right?" Yail shouted. "Help me," he said to someone else.

The bed moved as the wooden beam was levered off. Between the light and the dust, her eyes blinked repeatedly; then she closed them.

"Wait a minute, " Yail said. In a moment the bed bounced as he sat down on the edge. "Here. Hold your head back a little."

With his hand under her chin, she did as he said. Water washed over her face, warm and soothing.

"Open your eyes a little so the water can flush them out."

Keeping them open was difficult, but enough water got in to rinse much of the dust away. The air was still thick with it, making her cough. But it was better.

"What happened?" she asked.

"A bomb," he answered. He reached into a pocket and pulled out a handkerchief. "It seemed to be on the other side of the suite." She took the piece of linen and dabbed at her face.

"The other side of the suite? Sarah! Lucas!" She threw back the covers.

"Wait," Yail ordered, sensing her urgency. He searched through rubble on the floor a moment before lifting her slippers and shaking them off. "You'll need these."

She slipped the shoes on and jumped from the bed.

She ran down the hall, halfway through the great room, toward the bedroom Leila and Sarah had shared. Sheera intercepted her.

"No, Iroshi," she said, grabbing hold of her mentor's shoulders. "Don't go in there."

"Sheera. Get out of my way."

Beams of light danced in the dust coming from the room behind Sheera. Voices spoke softly and someone wailed.

"Sarah's dead." Sheera's voice broke and she cleared her throat. "Leila is alive but badly hurt."

"Ensi. Where is Lucas?"

Sheera looked alarmed at the tone in her voice and the words being spoken aloud.

We are trying, Iroshi. Stay quiet and give us time.

Dammit! This was no time to panic. Let Ensi do what he could. Sheera put a hand on her arm and tried to turn her back toward her own room. Iroshi shrugged her off.

"No! I must see Sarah and Leila."

"Iroshi, you're hurt. The guards and Mark are doing all they can. It will take a little while to get Leila freed. We will only get in the way."

"Erik?" she asked.

"I'm here, Iroshi," he answered from close behind. She realized that he was the one who had helped Yail with the beam, staying true to his responsibility to stay close.

Someone pushed open the sagging door of the suite behind him. Varia stepped into the room, amazingly dressed in all her official regalia, with two other councilors equally well dressed. The head of the Council rushed to Iroshi. Expressions of sadness and apology poured from her, but the expression on her face was fear. Did she fear Iroshi and the Glaive, or the new faction that was suddenly wreaking such havoc? Or both? That depended on which she thought could hurt her the most.

Angry words formed in her head but before she could shout them, Ensi yelled, *Iroshi!*

Her knees buckled. Ensi had never shouted at her like that. Both Sheera and Yail reached to support her.

Be quiet and let us work. If you don't calm yourself, we will lose Lucas for certain.

"What about Sarah?"

Too late. He was gone, and the emptiness felt greater than ever before. She took a deep breath, balled her hands into fists at her sides, then stretched the fingers out as far as they would go.

"Thank you, Varia, for coming," she said. "At the moment, we have work to do. Excuse me."

She turned to find Sheera blocking her path.

"It's all right."

Sheera stepped aside and Iroshi made her way into the shattered bedroom, Yail and the others following. The bed had collapsed under two beams, one from the wall behind the bed and one from the ceiling. The latter lay on top of the two women, pinning Leila alive and Sarah dead. Mark and three of the guards struggled to lift the massive wooden beam.

"Erik, help them," Iroshi ordered.

He hesitated. He could not concentrate on lifting the beam and protect Iroshi at the same time.

"It's all right, Erik," she said. "Nothing else will be tried today."

He nodded. With his help the beam was finally moved out of the way. A doctor and four medical aides took charge of Leila, who had fallen unconscious. Carefully, more than a dozen hands lifted her still form and placed her on a stasis stretcher. One of the aides activated the field that would hold her perfectly still without adding pressure to any injured point. The doctor and two aides wheeled her out. Iroshi motioned for Mark to follow. The other two aides helped remove Sarah's body.

"Sheera, is Varia still in the great room?" Iroshi asked.

Sheera nodded.

"Good. We'll need new quarters. Ask her to arrange for people to clean up this mess. We'll need all of Leila's and Sarah's personal things packed up."

She looked up through the broken roof. Stars winked in the black, early morning sky. As always. As if nothing had ever changed under their gaze. She choked back a sob. Too many things to do.

"Get maids, or whatever, to get everything packed up and moved into another suite," she went on. "Erik, you and I need to see if we can find what kind of explosive was used and how it was rigged. Maybe that will tell us something about who we're dealing with."

The brother nodded.

"Yail, if you have any experience with this sort of thing . . ."

"Not much," he said. "But I'd like to tag along. Just in case."

"All right. We'll start here, where the damage was worst."

While the two men began the search, Iroshi excused herself to put on clothes more suitable for the task than her silk pajamas. The soles of her slippers, although made of hard plastic, were ripped and torn from walking in broken glass and rubble. In her room, a maid was already at work packing her belongings, and she had to pull a pair of good boots out of a suitcase. By the time she had dressed and returned, Erik had found what was left of the bomb. It was the second of two connected by a length of wire in that wing of the suite, the first having gone off in the adjoining bedroom.

Following the connections, they found that the third bomb had been set in the great room. The next bomb had been set in the master bedroom but, somehow, the connection had come loose and the K35 explosive had not been ignited. The damage to Iroshi's room had come from destruction of the great room. Because of the loose connection, the room beyond hers, where Erik had been sleeping, was unharmed except for items overturned by the concussion.

For their own reasons, the assassins had chosen an insensitive, low explosive. That it was insensitive made sense if one had to carry it from one world to another in a ship. No use having something that could go off on its own at any moment. What seemed odd was the use of a low explosive. K35 had more of a heaving effect than a shock effect and, in this case, had caused several of the walls and ceilings of the suite to collapse. Essentially, it buried one in rubble rather than blowing one apart.

"It looks like the first three explosions caused the loose connection here," Iroshi said. Erik nodded agreement.

"K35 is not the best explosive to use in a sequential setup," he said.

She yawned and looked out the window. The sky was light, but the sun was not yet up.

"Well," she said, standing up and stretching. "I'm going over to the hospital and see how Leila is doing."

Yail stood beside her and put an arm around her waist.

"I think it's time you got some sleep," he said and started leading her toward the door.

"No, I must be there . . ."

"Sheera's with her. At the moment, there is nothing you can do to help," he said gently. "Let me get your cut taken care of . . ."

"What cut?"

"On your forehead."

She reached up, felt dried blood under her fingertips. The heat of his body pressed against her side.

"I promise to let you know as soon as Leila wakes up."

He maneuvered her through the broken doorway. Why was she letting him lead her away? There was so much work to do, so much to find out.

Erik started to follow.

"I'll take care of her," Yail said.

Erik stood with arms crossed and looked from him to Iroshi. Yail shrugged and led her outside, across the quadrangle to another wing of the palace complex, with Erik following at a distance. Inside, the great room was almost identical with the one that had been destroyed. Before it was destroyed, that is.

Oh, she was tired. A few hours' sleep would help.

"Ensi," she called. No answer. She took a quick breath at the pain in her soul. The chances of saving Lucas and Sarah . . .

Her hand made an involuntary fist. Please, gods, let him succeed.

Yail led her into the bathroom off the master bedroom, turned the water on in the shower, left and closed the door. She stripped, dropping her filthy clothes on the floor. The rushing water soothed her body but not her heart. She stood in danger of losing Lucas finally, irrevocably, and there was nothing she could do to prevent it. What good was it to be Iroshi of the Guild of the Glaive if she could not save her friends?

She turned off the water and stepped out. A pair of clean pajamas lay on the vanity, and she toweled dry and put them on. She went back into the bedroom, where Mark stood with Yail.

"Erik's getting some sleep and Johnson's with Sheera," Mark said. "I'll be right outside."

Iroshi nodded and the brother left. Yail came to her, took her hand, and led her to the bed.

"Do you need anything else?" he asked as he placed a bandage on her cut.

She shook her head and sat down on the edge of the bed.

"There is so much to do," she said. "But I . . ."

"Tomorrow," Yail said. "There is nothing that needs to be done this morning. You're tired and you need to sleep. You are only human."

"Yes," she said, fighting back tears. "Only human."

4

✦✦
✦

All of the rooms were identical. Furniture arranged the same; colors the same; windows the same; everything.

Leila was not in the corresponding room. She slept deeply in the room next to Iroshi's, hearing and feeling nothing. Her wounds had been tended. Except those of the heart. When she woke, that pain would be there, no less, no more than it had been. Only her drugged sleep kept it at bay for a time.

Iroshi released the pale hand, letting it lay back on the blanket. She stood and stretched, loosening tight muscles. It could not be more than half an hour since she had come in. No more than twelve hours since the explosion.

Another burning pyre day after tomorrow. Another spirit lost.

Lucas lost forever. And Sarah, who had just begun, so eager.

They should have known. As soon as they entered the rooms, they should have known that someone had been there while they were gone. But it did not work that way. A person had to have been within easy scanning distance for Ensi or one of the other companions to pick up any warning.

Not good enough! Especially now that they were
51

under attack. They had to know who was behind this and who worked with the group locally.

"Ensi, we start in-depth scanning right away," she said.

Her companion had been withdrawn all day. Very early in the morning, he and Janue had reported their failure. Then they left her to her memories and sorrow.

We touched him, Ensi had told her. *We heard him. It was just too sudden. Lucas is gone, Iroshi, and we can no longer reach him.*

She had cursed them, apologized, and cursed the gods. Then she had wept, crying out at everyone's impotence.

"With all our talents in the Glaive, we can't save this one life. Now there are two gone. What good are we? What good are our abilities if we can't save ourselves?"

We are not gods, Ensi had reminded her. *We suffer the same as all other people. Most of the time we survive. Perhaps longer than we should.*

"Lucas wanted to live. He looked forward to being a companion. He didn't want to die. We let him down."

She had collapsed on the bed and sobbed. Off and on during the day she had dozed, but sleep never took hold. At noon, she had gone into Leila's room. Sitting there, holding the young woman's hand, gave Iroshi the feeling of sharing grief, supporting one another.

But it was a false feeling. They both mourned a different person's passing. Different hopes and dreams; one with more experience and one with less.

"Ensi, answer me."

I am here.

"Have you and Janue had any success with the scanning?"

That is against the rules.

"I don't give a damn about the rules. This is a matter of survival. We must find the people who are trying to destroy the Glaive."

It may be that no one is trying to destroy the Glaive. Just keep us from interfering, as they see it, in some areas.

"They are trying to destroy us. Whoever they are. They have already killed two of our number. How many do they have to kill before you take this seriously?"

Dammit, why didn't he understand? The whole situation could get worse, and where would they be? Dead like Lucas and Sarah? Was that what it would take to make Ensi understand?

I am sorry. I simply do not think the situation is serious enough to warrant breaking our own rules. You formulated them yourself to safeguard . . .

"I know who formulated them and why. And I can break them."

Get ahold of yourself. Shouting aloud—or silently, for that matter—accomplished little. She took a deep breath.

"I want these people caught," she began quietly. "I want them punished. When we leave Galicia, I want all of this completed."

She was shouting again. She picked up an urn and threw it against the wall. It shattered, and she wondered if it was particularly valuable without caring.

"We will use every talent, ability, and trick we have to find these killers. And they will be punished, whether by legal means or by illegal means. I don't care. I will break every rule ever made to catch these people."

Mushimo and I . . .

"You got in touch with Mushimo? What right do you have to do such a thing behind my back?"

That was a stupid thing to say. He did not need her permission to contact anyone. But he did not need to bring everyone into this discussion!

"I can't believe you did that," she shouted.

She stopped, tried to catch her breath, which came in shallow gasps. She was furious, but that was totally irrational, and that made her even angrier. This was no good. Keep your head, my pretty, or lose it.

"Ensi, just start scanning, please," she said a little more calmly. "We have all this power in the Glaive, and we use so little of it. This time, I don't want to hold back. I want to show that the Glaive is a force to be reckoned with by everyone. Not just a few governments and corporations scattered around the galaxy. Just do it!"

She stood in the middle of her room, fists balled up at her sides, jaws so tight she was afraid they might lock that way. She closed her eyes tightly against more tears that oozed out anyway, their moist warmth turning cool as they trailed down her cheeks.

All right, Iroshi. We will do as you say.

The meeting had lasted six hours and twelve minutes. Yesterday's meeting lasted a total of twelve hours and fourteen minutes. Today's was the first dealing with the marriage. No one seemed to want to come to any agreement, and the thought had crossed Iroshi's mind that this proposed marriage might have been a ruse to lure a member of the Glaive to Galicia.

She sighed, hiding it behind her glass of tea. If paranoia set in, would it be blamed on her age, the stress of dealing with the current crisis, or both? Maybe . . . She almost shook her head. She had lost direction once before. Many years ago, doubt had arisen in her own mind about her ability to lead the Glaive. Although age had mellowed her, there were still times when she reacted in rage. At those times, it was difficult for reason to take over. Thank goodness, few people had ever witnessed those scenes. And Ensi was patient.

Another glance at the clock. Two more hours and it had to end. The cremation was scheduled at six.

"You have offered the seaside estate and a stable of terran horses for the daughter's hand," Jahn, the Vargas family representative, said. "Although *she* is not worthy, there is still no provision for the children of this union."

Jahn sat back in her chair and crossed her arms across her thin chest.

"We have no guarantee there will be any children. An examination has not been agreed to."

Garthon Walthen yawned. He seemed as bored as Iroshi was and had, so far, objected to nearly every offer that had been put forward. Strange, considering that the Vargas family was the more powerful and this alliance would be most beneficial to the Walthens. Yet, after recently rereading Lucas's research and reports, she was reminded that these kinds of negotiations were used by lesser families as an opportunity to claim power they did not otherwise possess.

Although this marriage would most likely take place, the negotiations would go on a while longer. This was their way. Lucas had become frustrated at the convoluted customs, and she found it equally exasperating. Of course, there were other important things to do not related to the marriage.

"The son is not worthy, either, but we know he can produce offspring," Garthon said.

"As can the daughter," Jahn said. She tossed a piece of paper onto the table. It had the appearance of a certificate of some kind. "An examination was made two days before this."

"Then let things proceed," Garthon said heartily, leaning forward.

At last! The betrothed couple would meet and bed, and if she became pregnant they would wed. All Lucas had accomplished before his death was make arrangements for the examination of the daughter, after convincing the Vargas faction that it was time and that the girl was worth the cost of the examination and the fertility pills. Not much was left to chance in dynastic marriages on Bosque.

"What would the Vargas family consider a fair offer for the children of this marriage?" Iroshi asked. "It must be no more than enough for their upkeep and to divide between them when they come of age."

"Since the children will be more worthy than their parents, we would be proud if Walthen Mining were set aside for their benefit."

"Impossible!" Garthon shouted. He jumped to his feet and made as if to leave the table. With a loud exhalation, he sat back down, then stared at his hands folded together on the table.

"There are other children to consider. And grandchildren—some of which are already born—to think of," he said.

Start high and work your way down. That was the way these things were handled here. Everything bargained for, everyone first claiming what they held was unworthy, then asking for an exorbitant price.

They continued haggling for another half an hour. Iroshi entered pleas for reasonableness every so often, first from one side, then the other. Gradually, they came closer and closer until finally it was done.

"A celebration in honor of this day," Garthon said.

Since the daughter's family had to pay for the examination, the son's family paid for the prenuptial banquet.

"Right here, tonight," Garthon continued, then he paused. "Iroshi, I am sorry. I forgot your sad duty later today. We will postpone the celebration for a day or two. We specifically want to show you our thanks for helping bring these negotiations to a happy end."

"Tomorrow, then?" she suggested.

Best not to drag this out, so that the more important things could be seen to. Such as finding Lucas's killers and punishing them. It was good to be able to consider that coldly rather than with hot rage.

After the cremation ceremony, Yail accompanied her to her suite. She waved him to follow into her bedroom.

"Is there any news?" she asked.

"None yet," he replied. "Only possibilities. The police have not moved on the two men. They are keeping them under surveillance, however, so that they do not disappear. At this point, there is no choice. They must do everything to at least keep up the appearance of cooperation."

"And the man I described to you?"

"There are no records of such a man, either as a native of Galicia or as a visitor."

"He is the key. I know it."

"How do you know it?" he asked.

Ensi had sensed that the young man puzzled over the ways in which Iroshi or the Glaive could have gotten the names of the same two men he had identified, and a description of a third one. Not one possible explanation had come to him except the Glaive's having spies on Bosque, something she had downplayed. He still suspected spies only because that was the only way he could conceive of. How would one explain that the information was the last thing gleaned from Lucas's memories after he died? Before he died a second time . . .

"Ensi, are there still no signs that Yail might be a danger to us?"

None. I am beginning to suspect that he would like to become a member of the Glaive. He often worries about the lack of opportunities here in Galicia in his chosen profession. His superiors find him a little too freewheeling for their liking.

"Maybe that would be possible. But not so soon after losing Sarah."

Thoughts of the girl brought more recent memories of the cremation and deeper losses that could not be spoken of. Tears came to her eyes, and she fought them back.

Yail took her hand and kissed the palm. Chills raced through her body. Suddenly she wanted very much to be held and comforted. For an instant she would have given anything for him—or someone she could trust—to take all the responsibility off her shoulders. That would never happen, of course. Ultimately, she was in charge and would dare anyone to forget that. Everyone who knew her never dared.

Yail slid closer to her on the sofa. He slipped an arm around her shoulder.

"I am so sorry about Sarah," he said. "I wish there was something I could do to help."

He was a damn mind reader! And his compassion brought back tears that could no longer be controlled. They spilled warmly down her cheeks. She rubbed at the streaks with the heel of her hand. He took her hand again, held it a moment, then kissed the palm. She let him pull her head to his breast.

"You don't always have to be Iroshi of the Glaive," he said softly.

No, I am a woman, and women cry and need warmth and tenderness.

She sobbed, and he held her close. His warmth gave comfort and took the edge off the bitterness. Anger would not be so easily pushed aside, but soon the sobs ceased. She did not push away from him. For tonight at least, let the woman be treated tenderly and let Iroshi of the Glaive rest from her responsibilities. They kissed, and for a while the pain went away.

5

✦

The meeting room was different, and this time the meeting itself was not going well. Commissioner Gretzh resented Iroshi's interference. His posture indicated that much, and when Ensi probed his thoughts, his anger was nearly palpable.

At the moment, the commissioner sat across the conference table with his arms folded across his chest and his chin sticking out. Just one blow would put that chin back in proper perspective.

Iroshi, such thoughts are counterproductive.

"I know. But just once . . ."

No use finishing the thought. What was important now was to understand why he would ignore the information they had given him regarding the identities of two men involved in the murder. She glanced once at poor Yail sitting to one side, literally and figuratively between a professional superior and his lover and current assignment. His attitude clearly showed that he favored her side in this discussion, but he recognized that antagonizing Gretzh would do no one any good.

"Commissioner Gretzh," she began again. "I am sorry if we have given you cause for anger. We of the Glaive only wish to bring Lucas Kent's killers to justice. He was our friend and our colleague and was here for no purpose other than to negotiate a marriage."

"We understand your concern, Iroshi," he said in his baritone voice. That much, at least, was pleasant about the man. "We only wish you would go away and let us do our job. This is not the first murder we have investigated."

"I understand that, sir. However, we have certain talents and resources that might be of use in the investigation, as evidenced by those names we gave you."

The man puffed up even more, if that was possible. His face could not get any redder. She had never run into such a stone wall before. Clearly the reality of cooperation in this matter was not equal to the words of the Council.

Give it up for now, Iroshi. I think we can only make him angrier.

"There must be a way to gain his cooperation."

Perhaps later. For now, I suggest we work alone.

"Perhaps you're right. This whole discussion has been a trial." To Gretzh she said, "Again, I am sorry if we have offended, Commissioner. I will not bother you any more on this matter at this time. But we would appreciate it if you would question these two men and think about accepting our help."

He nodded and remained in his seat when Iroshi rose to go. Yail led the way outside, and once they were in the street he complained bitterly about the actions of the head of the planetary agency. A minute into his tirade, he stopped suddenly and turned to her. She stopped, too, ready to listen further. Other pedestrians were forced to give them a wide berth by the surrounding phalanx of capital guards.

"I am sorry, Iroshi. I know that I should show more loyalty. If it had been anyone but you . . . But that does not excuse my outburst."

The formality of the speech caught her off guard, and for a moment she could think of nothing to say. She had been thinking that his words, although inappropriate, had to be inspired by his feelings for her. One of the basic operating principles within the Glaive was to show loyalty to one's employer, even though the arrangements were always temporary. But, then, her own reaction had been belligerent.

"Please excuse me," he said. "I should go to my apartment and try to calm myself."

"Of course," she said, and he strode off. The guards gave way, then closed ranks again.

Something is bothering him, Ensi commented.

"I know. He isn't usually so impulsive. I suppose you can't find out what it is?"

Of course I can. I already have. He's falling in love with you.

"That isn't funny."

No, it is not, when you have no intention of carrying this affair any further.

Yail disappeared around a corner, and she turned back to the road leading to the palace complex. The Greer brothers fell in behind; the palace guards were spread around the general area.

She sighed. The situation was neither funny nor simple. For either of them. Her great curse was that she always fell in love. Casual affairs were not her forte, to say the least.

Why do you persist in having these emotional involvements? I thought we were done with them for a time.

"We were, I suppose. There have been fewer since Mitchell came into my life. And never any involvement with someone within the Glaive. You know that."

I think it must be due to your father's abandoning you and . . .

"Please, don't psychoanalyze me. I'm the way I am, and I don't intend to change this late in life."

Even though it causes you great pain.

"It also gives me great ecstasy, equal to the pain in every way."

Ensi withdrew. He and Janue were going to seek out and scan the two men from the mob. He would not begin until Iroshi was safely within the walls of the palace, while Janue, more of a free agent, was working steadily. Lucas's erstwhile companion needed to keep his thoughts from turning inward too often. Ensi said he talked with him about Lucas's death but was not ready to face anyone else. He suspected that revenge was a strong incentive for his dedication. Without stating it specifically, he was worried that she might try to do something to the men. No one was sure that they could stop her if she tried. Iroshi was not sure he would want to.

They had reached the gateway into the palace compound. Like the buildings within, it and the surrounding wall shone white in the mid-morning sun. Photographers and newspeople surrounded her and her party as they approached.

"Iroshi, is it true that you've found Lucas's killer?" someone shouted from the crowd. Other questions were shouted, each voice drowning out the others. Right in the forefront stood Grace Lewis of Interstellar News. That journalistic abomination was something Iroshi and the Glaive would have to take some blame for, since they had contributed both credits and time to promoting long-distance communication. Titus Jones, an entrepreneur on Tylus IV, had picked up on the technology and reinvented the old news networks. Biggest thing going on some worlds.

Biggest nuisance—along with all the other news organizations—at the moment.

The Greer brothers and the palace guards swept her through the crowd and the gate with little effort. Once inside, and with the gate closed between her and the still-shouting crowd, she turned and considered them.

"They're getting faster, Ensi."

Yes, and that could work for or against us.

"In the present situation or in the future?"

Yes.

She hated it when he got cute, and she told him so. He chuckled, then withdrew. In another moment they had entered the suite. Iroshi went straight to her room and stripped down, wiping sweat from her body with the soiled jumpsuit, which she threw into the cleaner. Thank goodness the Galicians liked all the conveniences. She practiced for a while, but her heart was not in it. The investigation was going nowhere, and frustration increased as she was stymied at every turn. Obviously these people were not well enough understood to be maneuvered her way successfully. Nor did they have the respect for the Glaive that she was accustomed to after twenty-three years.

Maybe that was where the news media would be useful. A few well-chosen words planted by someone from within the Glaive . . . Better yet, a native of Galicia. Would it be fair to use Yail? Probably not, but what better bait could there be? Let the woman from Interstellar News find out he was involved with Iroshi of the Glaive, and she would be all over him.

No, he could not be sent in cold. He would have to be rehearsed, even convinced, to betray her. If his admiration and affection for her were genuine.

However, the truth would serve. If Galicia would not assist in the investigation, perhaps Aulda would. Not by crossing jurisdictions, and all that. But they could hinder, even cancel, the marriage negotiations if Aulda saw Galicia's lack of help as an embarrassment, thus making the new seal on the alliance less desirable. It could be hinted that the Glaive was considering some action of their own regarding the murder.

They must move carefully. Keeping things from heating up too much might be as difficult as getting them heated up in the first place.

"Ensi."

Yes.

"Scan."

Iroshi relaxed and let him read her thoughts up to that point. One of the things that made bonding work so well was how thoroughly the companion could withdraw, or the ability of the host to erect a barrier for privacy.

Everyone needs privacy once in a while. However, on those rare occasions when he withdrew completely—was not there—the feeling was one of such utter loneliness that they seldom parted in that way.

It is feasible, he said after a moment. *We must be wary. The news media are sometimes difficult to manipulate successfully. They are so greedy.*

"I think Grace Lewis is the best one to contact."

She certainly has a wider network. However, she isn't stupid and could suspect that Yail is a plant.

"He's too innocent for her to suspect, I think. Then again, that innocence might work against his being convincing."

Could he carry it off without giving too much away? No sense taking chances; her first instinct to not let him know what was going on was probably good. Just give him the information and let Grace go for it. Poor guy. He was going to be eaten alive.

If he finds out that you have used him in this way, it will ruin your relationship with him.

"I know. I simply can't think of any other way to accomplish it. If he knows everything, he just won't be able to pull it off. He's too honest and naive."

You could ask him.

"The way he seems to feel about me, he'd be willing to try anything."

He loves you, but he has not let that cloud his ambition. He sees his relationship with you as a means to getting off this world, possibly as a member of the Glaive.

"You scanned him, then."

Of course. Anything that has a strong influence on you and the work—or anyone—is carefully considered. I always have before, and you know it.

"But you said he had some kind of natural block against scanning."

Even he lets his guard down at times.

Iroshi thought back to the few times she and Yail had made love. The emotional impact had been greater than she had expected, adding much to the physical pleasure. Yet they had not been alone after all.

"When were you going to tell me this?"

I hoped never.

She fussed for a while, and Ensi remained silent, perhaps not even listening. It was hard to tell. Eventually she ran out of pique, and they seriously discussed how to handle the accidental information leak. Iroshi decided to go with Ensi's feelings and tell Yail what they wanted done and see if he agreed.

Yail did not come back that night. Later, as Iroshi lay sleepless, she wondered how she could have missed seeing the possibility of telepathy in Yail. Even when she was in love, she was more sensitive to the kind of person the partner was than that. Of course, he could have kept her from seeing deeply if what Ensi said was true. After all, she could not actually read minds. Not like Ensi could.

Next morning, Yail's composure was almost alarming. He sat in a chair in the living room, coolly considering what Iroshi had asked of him. The thoughts swirled in his brain almost visibly: in essence, if he felt like it, he could betray his own people—just a little—and get the officials to cooperate in the investigation.

If he chose to help her, he would do it for ambition or love. If he chose not to help, he would do it out of loyalty. Which choice would make him the more honorable man in his own eyes?

Was that the question he was asking himself at that moment? Or was he asking which would make him the most honorable in her eyes? She did not even know the answer to that. Particularly since he had already taken her side at least once.

Strange how events could progress in an unperceived direction. It had never been her intention to use his attraction to her, not in this way. Or any similar way. That he had volunteered to help get the investigation moving had shown a certain honesty.

He looked up and their eyes met.

He is having difficulty making up his mind. That is all I can tell.

"This is unfair," Iroshi said aloud. "We have no right to put you in this position, Yail. I withdraw the request."

She stood up, went to the bar, and refilled her glass. Her hand shook a little, giving a real jolt of surprise. This whole situation was getting on her nerves badly, and she really did feel regret at putting Yail in this position. The dark tea swirled in her glass, and for once she wished for something stronger.

"*I* came to you," he said. "That first time. I hated the way you were being put off, all the red tape and stonewalling. I hated knowing that officials of my government were being manipulated by some outside group.

I'm still not sure who they are. I was hoping that you could help me find out."

"Are you so sure the manipulation is coming from outside your own government?" she asked.

"I have no proof, but yes, I am."

"Are you saying that you want to go through with the plan I just outlined?"

Iroshi left the bar and sat back down opposite him.

"I guess I am. It looks even more like I'm betraying Galicia, and that worries me."

"It should."

"I know." Yail pushed back the lock of hair that habitually fell out of place. "I've gotten in over my head, haven't I?"

"A little, maybe." She moved to sit beside him and took his hand between hers. "Whatever you decide to do, make sure that you are able and want to see it through. I won't think any less of you if you want to drop the whole thing right now. However, your own people may think less of you if they find out you aided the Glaive in this."

"True enough." He sighed and squeezed her hand. "I think I realize more than any of them how much bigger this problem is." He turned to face her, lifted her hand to his lips. "The only thing I ask is that we not reveal the truth about you and me. My family would disown me."

"Why on Nevas would they do that?"

"You are not of a sufficiently important family." He managed to look sheepish.

"And?" she prompted. He turned his gaze to his lap.

"And . . . I . . . They would consider you . . ."

". . . too old," she finished. He nodded without raising his head. She laughed and patted his hand.

"It doesn't bother me," she assured him. "I never thought of our relationship as a permanent one, no matter how things turn out. I am flattered by your affection, and I hope you are flattered by mine. However, I have a life mate back on Rune-Nevas, as I told you. Our being separated so often makes finding comfort in others' arms needful."

He looked up then with what might have been a hurt expression in his eyes. Although she had told him about Mitchell very early on, what she had just said might make him feel as if he was only a momentary dalliance in her eyes.

"I don't admit just anyone to my bed," she said. "In fact, you are the first in many years."

That made him look happier. She kissed him long and slow, their tongues touching, dancing in and out. If only there was time . . . When they parted, she got to her feet.

"I have some work to do," she said. "Don't do anything about this little plan until you hear from me."

He nodded. "Me, too. I'll be back in an hour or so."

He kissed her cheek and left. His scent lingered around her, and it was nice to stand a moment and breathe it in.

Iroshi, Ensi called. He sounded unusually excited.

"What is it?"

Janue and I were searching as you said. Something has happened.

"What?"

The off-worlder, Carson, has been found. Gretzh and his men have him in custody.

"Why have they arrested him now?"

I . . . That is, we . . .

"What did you do?"

Well, we did not like this plan with the news media and Yail so we took matters into our own hands, so to speak.

"Yes?"

We found Carson in a local bar. You remember the ghosts we presented to you in the temple? We just showed Carson the same ones. When he started fighting the air, the manager called the police. The authorities then had no choice but to take him into custody.

"Let's go," she said, picking up her jacket and sword. "Contact Mark and have him get hold of Yail. Tell him to meet us there."

She and her guards nearly ran all the way. It was the first time that she resented the fact that ground transportation was banned from the city's streets. Still, they arrived at the headquarters building quickly enough. The Commissioner's face showed shock when she marched into his office. He leapt to his feet.

"How dare you barge into my office?" he blustered.

"I dare, Commissioner. I understand that you've arrested Carson at last."

"How did you . . ."

"Has he been questioned yet?"

"We just . . ."

"Good. I will be there when you do."

She put on her best smile and sat down in a chair facing the now red-faced policeman.

"After all," she continued, "that's the least you can do, isn't it? When do we begin?"

"They were ghosts," Carson said, fear still edging his voice.

He had answered none of their questions, instead describing what he'd seen in the bar. With Erik beside her, Iroshi stood to one side, arms crossed, watching and listening. In spite of their best efforts, the interrogators had been unable to get the man to focus on their questions about the mob and murder.

He is still genuinely frightened, Ensi reported. *However, he's using that to hide behind, to avoid their questions.*

"We had better step in, then," Iroshi answered. Aloud, she said, "Gentlemen, if you will let me, I think I can get Mr. Carson's attention."

Across the room, Gretzh dropped his arms and took a step forward. "I don't think . . ." he began.

"Clearly, your tactics are not working," she said. "As I've said before, we of the Glaive have other means of interrogation. No, not torture," she added hastily, silencing the Commissioner's protest. "Just other means."

She moved to stand before the prisoner.

"If you gentlemen could give Erik and me a little time alone with him."

Carson's eyes narrowed as he finally looked up at her.

"You can't do that," he said. "She isn't on the police force."

Gretzh exhaled loudly and motioned for his men to leave the room.

"It can't hurt anything to let you try, I suppose," he said. He started out, too, then turned back. "If I find one mark on him . . ."

"Not to worry, Commissioner. He will be returned to you in fine shape."

He does not believe you will have any better luck.

"I thought that was the case. He wouldn't leave me here if he did. How is our prisoner now?"

More afraid than ever. He knows this is not normal procedure.

"Not by a long shot."

She smiled at Carson.

"Well, Mr. Carson. Alone at last. You were saying something about ghosts a moment ago."

A man appeared dressed in a kilt, holding a claymore in both hands.

"Did he look anything like this?"

Carson squealed and pushed back into his chair.

"That's a powerful-looking sword, isn't it, Mr. Carson? I have a feeling that he's probably very good with a weapon like that. Shall we see?"

"No! Please. Keep him away from me."

"If you don't tell me what we want to know about the murder of Lucas Kent, I am going to let this fine specimen of a man slice off your head. He's not going to cut you up a little at a time. You have just one chance to save yourself."

The claymore rose overhead, the man's biceps bulging with the effort.

"No! I'll talk. I'll talk."

6

Do you remember the terrible row on Akkad VII?
About the slavers?

Iroshi walked along the same path back to the palace
complex. Yail walked at her side and the usual cadre of
guards surrounded her. Moving from one place to another like this was becoming tedious. Well, it could not
be helped.

"Of course. The Glaive refused to witness the contract
between the Donnington Corp. and the government on
Akkad VII. The contract appeared at first to be for the
transport of paid laborers for the harvest. However, it
turned out that the laborers were actually indentured
slaves. It was our first encounter with the trade."

Reciting the facts helped to anchor the memory. However, what this had to do with Carson and his bosses was
still a mystery.

And the final outcome on that deal?

"You know as well as I do that it all fell through.
Donnington lost a great deal of money. Akkad VII
nearly went bankrupt when most of their cash crops died
on the vine." She snapped her fingers. A couple of the
guards cut their eyes toward her, but the rest ignored the

sound. They were becoming accustomed to her eccentricities.

"Donnington disappeared. As far as we've been able to tell, no one has heard one word from any officer or employee of the company."

Until now.

"What does that have to do with Mr. Carson and this Walker woman he works for?"

Rhea Walker is the wife of Duncan Walker, chief stockholder and managing director of Donnington Corp. Rather, she is the widow. He died two years ago, apparently a suicide.

"Who was the truthsayer sent to witness that contract?"

It was . . . Lucas. That whole deal fell through more than four years before. Is it possible that this Walker woman has held a grudge that long but done nothing until now?

She thought a moment.

"Was Lucas requested for the assignment here on Bosque?"

No.

"Could they have somehow known that he would be sent? There is no set rotation. We select truthsayers and warriors both on an as-needed and an as-qualified basis."

I know how they are selected, Ensi said a little testily.

"Sorry, I was just going over everything to remind myself. Trying to find some way . . . They couldn't have known he would be sent. Maybe it didn't matter who was sent. Maybe Lucas's being here was a coincidence."

I don't believe much in coincidences.

"Neither do I. We'll have to dig deeper. Have you gotten a fix on her yet?"

No. I managed to glean a little information when we first scanned Carson. She is here on Bosque. Carson is afraid of her.

"Not as afraid of her as he is of us. And the ghosts."

He is most afraid of whoever is nearest. It seems odd that anyone would trust him with any information at all.

Yail glanced at her occasionally out of the corner of his eye. His thoughts had been in flux ever since Carson's confession. According to Ensi, the young officer wondered how she had managed it while, at the same time, his admiration had grown immensely. The latter was also due, in part, to her telling him it would no longer be necessary to set up the newspeople.

Speaking of whom, there was not a trace of any of them at the gates. That was a relief. The Glaive party entered their wing with no hindrances. Although Carson's interrogation had been easy enough, Iroshi was tired. It *was* one more hurdle overcome, another point of tension relieved. Everything could proceed, now that the police had their prisoner and everything he knew of the plot.

"Maybe I need to leave Galicia," Yail said suddenly. "Maybe I just can't learn enough here." He shook his head and turned to her. "I don't know how you got Carson to talk, or how you and the Glaive do the things you do. But I'm not going to learn that here in Galicia."

Erik held the door to the suite open while they entered the great room. He went toward his own room, leaving them alone.

Iroshi kissed Yail lightly, then pulled away. He sounded so young, and she felt guilt and longing all at once.

"You are still very young," she said. "And there are a lot of things happening in your life right now. Large and small. All demanding your attention, all better handled if you could give each one your full attention. I'm sorry that I have added to all of this."

"I'm not," he said. "I am so glad you came into my life, even if for a short while."

He kissed her so sweetly that her heart cried out. She led him into the bedroom. Each time together was a learning experience for them both: Yail, young and enthusiastic; Iroshi, older and experienced. Afterward, he lay propped up on one elbow, brushing the hair away from her face.

"I love you," he said huskily.

Her heart skipped a beat. Not an unexpected profession, but one she had hoped would not be made. The last thing she wanted to do was hurt him.

"I know you love the man you are bonded to," he went on when she remained silent.

"Yes, I do. For many years now." She smoothed the furrows from his forehead with her fingertips. "I am neither your first love nor your last."

He smiled and kissed her. "Don't worry," he said. "I won't ask for any promises. But men do dream, too."

She laughed. "I know. And I'm glad to be part of your dreams for now."

Someone knocked on the door.

"Yes?" Iroshi said.

"There's trouble, Iroshi," Erik said through the door. "Carson's been killed."

Garthon Walthen paced behind his side of the table while railing at Tarek Varia. He had been going like that for nearly five minutes. He was more upset by Carson's murder than anyone else.

Iroshi had thus far been amazed by the Auldan representative's reaction, ranting and at the same time intimating that he could hardly be blamed for his reaction. After all, his country's indirect hope had been for an alliance with an equally strong government. The Auldans had no desire to carry the burden for both, either now or in the future. Everything she said had fueled Walthen's ire, no matter how innocently she phrased it.

Or, seemingly innocently. Every word was carefully considered for just that effect. When all events were considered more dispassionately at some later time, it must never seem that she or the Glaive had contributed to this dispute. It must always appear to have been a natural reaction to an ill-handled murder investigation that resulted in the death of the prime suspect while every news organization of the known worlds watched.

"Every network!" Walthen shouted, stopping to pound a fist on the table. "If this matter is not cleared up soon, there will be no marriage. That I promise you."

He glared around the table at friend and foe alike, gathered his robes around him, and sat down. He mopped at his reddened face with a white linen handkerchief, and after a moment he stopped panting from the exertion. He was a big man, and carrying all that weight back and forth had cost him quite a bit of energy.

"But the banquet and . . ." Jahn Vargas began. She was cut off by Tarek Varia.

"Mr. Walthen, I assure you that we are doing everything we can," Varia said. "We are pursuing the matter with the cooperation of Iroshi and the Guild of the Glaive. I contacted the Commissioner just this afternoon, and more officers are being assigned to the case. A new lead has surfaced."

"Ensi, did you catch that?" Iroshi asked.

Yes. We had intercepted the information when she received it a few minutes ago. For the moment they are rehashing what we and they already knew. However, they do seem to be working harder—shall we say—than they were. We are in as close contact as possible.

"Good. I want to know if they get anywhere near Walker. I want to get to her before the police if possible.

"Can you read the Commissioner, or is he too far away?"

He is projecting pretty strongly right now. He believes you are somehow responsible for what has happened.

"He's more clever than I gave him credit for."

"I am glad that progress is being made," Walthen responded to Varia's report. "However, until this matter is concluded, the marriage negotiations will cease." He rose, followed by his entourage of five. "Iroshi," he said and bowed to her. "I am sorry that your efforts on our behalf have been derailed in this manner. I hope you understand."

She stood and bowed her head. "I am sorry, Mr.

Walthen, that events have come to this impasse. However, please understand that knowing you are not comfortable with continuing at this time, I would not try to dissuade you."

"Thank you," he said, turned on his heel, and left the meeting room. Varia and the Galician contingent had risen also, but received no farewell from the departing dignitaries. She scowled at their departing backs, but managed to replace the expression with a more pleasant one before facing Iroshi.

"I, too, apologize, Iroshi," she said. "I don't know why this incident has angered the Auldans so."

"Don't worry, Varia. If we move quickly to bring the investigation to a close, everything will proceed as planned. I am sorry that the marriage must be put off; however, I do appreciate your efforts, and those of your police, in finding the murderers."

After a few more pleasantries, Iroshi rushed back to her suite. While the meeting had dragged on, Ensi had informed her that information had been found regarding the instigator of the attack.

"Where did you find her?" she asked while Mark and Erik listened in through their own companions.

The three of them sat in the living room of the suite. Mark poised on the edge of one of the sofas as if ready for flight. Erik lounged in the chair in the corner. Iroshi sat back against the corner of the second sofa. Tension ran up and down her spine like a guitar riff.

She has not left the port or her ship. As you wanted, we scanned minds. Mark and Erik alternately worked their way through the city. Until we found someone not from this world. No empathic or telepathic abilities are apparent.

"Have you confirmed that this anti-Glaive movement was a ruse?"

Yes, she and her organization were behind it all along. Not that it isn't a threat. Those who have joined have a genuine fear of the Glaive.

"How would they react if they found out their founder dealt in slaves?"

Few people care about that. Most do not believe that slavery exists anymore. Technically, it doesn't. Those people are not bought and sold, only a few of their years.

"Yes, from the day they sign the papers until they die. The places they go . . . Who would voluntarily work on some of those worlds?"

You are preaching to the converted, Iroshi.

"I know. Do you have details of her plans?"

No. I had to back away.

"She detected you? I thought you said she had no extrasensory abilities."

She felt uneasiness at the very least. Whether or not she figures out what happened or that the Glaive was at the root, I cannot say.

"Who else would she think you were from?"

She spoke aloud, "Mark. Erik. Any ideas on what to do?"

So far the brothers had shown no discontent at being treated as simple guards. However, that was unfair to them. They were, after all, full members of the Glaive and had every right to be consulted, especially since they were on the scene. She certainly would have consulted . . .

She shook off the thought, but not before Lucas's name flashed through her mind. *Keep that up, and you will end up in the proverbial padded cell,* she thought. Ensi remained quiet.

"We need to pick up this Walker woman," Erik said. "Or somehow get whatever information she has."

Mark nodded. "Not only to find out what threat to the Glaive may remain," he added, "but also to make sure that threat no longer extends to you, Iroshi."

There was a frightening thought. Not that the threat extended to her. No, not that. What was frightening was that Mark—and possibly Erik, too—thought of a threat to her in personal terms.

That should not surprise you.

"Of course it does," she responded silently. "I didn't know what I was doing all these years. Next thing someone will do is erect a statue in my honor so everyone can worship at my feet."

Don't be so paranoid. They honor you; they do not worship you. Not yet. Maybe never.

"I've been thinking of ways to keep this thing from getting out of hand. When I die . . ."

Ensi cringed. She felt it, deep within her spirit. The prospect upset him, at least. Terrified him, at worst. The first indication of the effect of Lucas's death.

"We'll leave that for later." Aloud, she said, "How far do you think we should go to get information from Walker?"

"I wouldn't hold back," Erik said. "Walker has done

her best to create a paranoia against the Glaive. Such a paranoia would be dangerous enough. Creating it as a front actually gives us two sources of danger."

Mark nodded agreement.

You cannot risk tearing apart her mind. We have come too far to start disregarding the rules.

"I haven't accepted their ideas, Ensi. Not totally, anyway. I just don't see any other way."

She thanked the brothers for their advice. Mark remained while Erik went about his other business; always within calling distance, however.

Only once had she felt such a personal threat. Then, she had been so confined, so besieged, but that had been a matter of hours. Although it had seemed that the mind vampire had pursued her for days. She shuddered. The memory was nearly as strong as ever. Only its frequency had changed. For months after the attack, she had remembered. In dreams. In sudden flashes while awake. Eventually the dreams went away. The flashes came infrequently until they stopped altogether. Now they were returning.

Was she doomed to remember every time there was a serious threat? If so, her work could be doomed.

This matter must be brought to an end!

"Ensi."

Yes.

"You remember the maze? The one the creature built in my mind?"

I could not forget that.

"What if we used the same technique on Walker? If

she has no telepathic abilities, the effect would be different . . ."

You were just remembering how devastating that attack was. How could you even think of doing the same thing to another person?

"It's a shortcut. A means of solving this problem."

I know the memory has returned, that it haunts you. However, we cannot use such methods. Think of the reputation of the Glaive. We have worked for over twenty years to establish the organization as an honorable one. Our people can be trusted with any assignment we accept. And we do not accept any police assignments. Or military ones.

We are bodyguards and truthsayers. Leave the police work to those who know it best. We can assist with information, but we must not lose sight of our purpose.

"How can we achieve our purpose when the Glaive is threatened and attacked with impunity?"

You are afraid, and that is only natural. Rise above that.

"I'm not afraid . . ."

A sudden clamor exploded outside. Mark jumped to his feet. Erik ran into the great room. The door burst open and Yail rushed in.

"We're under attack," he said breathlessly.

"How many?" Iroshi asked.

"Thirty, maybe. Too many."

From the sounds coming from outside, they were using swords. She had expected nothing but guns, even though they were a scarce commodity on Bosque.

"How are you with a sword?" she asked as she hurried into the bedroom.

"I know how," he answered, following behind.

She pulled her katana from its scabbard where it lay on the dresser, then pointed at a case sitting on the floor.

"There should be one to your liking in there."

Without waiting until he chose a weapon, she rushed back into the living room. The brothers stood on either side of the door with their weapons drawn.

"Let's go," she ordered.

7

Blood pounded in her ears. Her heart sang with the first clang of her sword striking another. Within three strokes she had found the void—or it had found her. She was one with the sword, knowing nothing of her surroundings, knowing everything. She was one with her opponent—a woman, larger than she but moving without grace.

The cut across the woman's abdomen—she felt that too, but without the pain. The surprise and sorrow stung. Always two sides, opposites. Reward and punishment. Good and bad. A price must be paid.

The next opponent—a man—had fear in his eyes. He faced Iroshi, ronin, warrior, Glaive master. He *should* be afraid.

She knocked his sword aside with her blade. The tip circled, thrust. Crimson formed on his beige shirt, widening as he dropped to his knees.

A man's voice cried out as a capital guard's gun found a mark. Another cry from behind. Iroshi turned, saw Yail. He knew how to use the sword, but not well. His opponent was better and had cut the young policeman's left forearm. She started to step in, but another man moved between.

He was not afraid. The saber did not waver. Clearly a man who thought he could take Iroshi.

She lunged forward in the traditional kendo charge: right foot pounding the ground, pulling the rest of her after. Saber defended confidently. He dodged to one side and attacked. Her turn to defend. He swung, thrust, letting the heavier sword work against her, not letting it work against him.

His movements were untrained but effective. Probably he was self-trained. He knew nothing of the void or zen. The differences made them equally matched. As they moved back and forth she sank farther into the void. His movements brought pleasure and pain through the warrior's red haze. His next move would be to swing from her right to her left. Instead of blocking the blow, she turned the katana to push his blade faster in its sweep, then thrust. The point entered his body just under the sternum. First he looked surprised, then resigned. Blood ran down the polished steel, nearly reaching the tsuba. She pulled it free, and Saber swayed a moment before collapsing.

The wound was fatal, straight to the heart. She remembered Yail, turned in a circle but could not find him. Guns fired at fleeing backs. An answering shot struck the wall just behind her. Reinforcements from the capital guards pursued along with some of those who had been guarding the building wing.

Iroshi straightened, letting the red haze fade, leaving the void. Yail stood before her, holding his left forearm with his right hand. Blood oozed between his fingers.

"Someone get a doctor," she said.

Yail smiled, and she took the sword from where it hung in his left hand. Mark and Erik stood close by, sure that she was all right and that they had won. She handed Yail's sword to Mark.

"Let the guards take care of these," she said, pointing at the bodies. A woman moaned, the only indication that any of them was alive.

Eleven casualties, none of them her people. Two guardsmen lay among the bodies, one dying, the other dead. The rest, attackers.

"All locals," Yail said from beside her. "I don't understand how they got through the gate."

"Capital security will have to be investigated," Iroshi said. "Clearly, there are some weaknesses."

An hour later, she sat in the living room discussing that subject with Varia. Yail sat at the other end of the sofa, his arm bandaged. The Greers stood a short distance behind, clearly making the Chief Councilor nervous where she sat on the opposite sofa.

"Please believe me, Iroshi," Varia said. "We are doing everything possible to strengthen security within the capital complex."

"It's a little late, Madame Councilor," Iroshi said. "This is the second attack on me and my party. Terrorists are getting inside your complex on a fairly regular basis."

"Well, there weren't any problems until you and your Glaive came to Galicia."

Yail shot a quick glance at Iroshi, which she ignored.

"You think we brought this violence to you, then. Even though we came at your express invitation." She stood. "In that case, it might be best if we leave." She turned to the brothers. "Contact the racer crews and have them prepare for . . ."

"Please, Iroshi!" Varia jumped to her feet. "I only meant that we have no experience in dealing with problems like this."

"Do you think we do? Nothing like this happens on Rune-Nevas. Nor do we have similar problems on any other world. Lucas came here as a truthsayer, not a warrior. We are here because of his death and stayed at your request to conclude Lucas's work."

She walked around the sofa, placed the palms of her hands on the back.

"If we do not resolve the matter of Lucas's murder soon—and that of this Carson—we will leave Bosque. If there is another attack on us, we will leave Bosque. In either case, the marriage will probably never take place."

She stood straight and crossed her arms.

"Now. Do we get your total cooperation?" Varia nodded. "Good. We are sending for several more Glaive members, warriors . . ."

Iroshi, Ensi broke in suddenly. *She is leaving.*

"Walker?" Iroshi asked silently.

Yes.

Aloud, she said, ". . . and truthsayers. If you will pardon us, we will start making preparations."

Varia frowned at the dismissal, but she and the two councilors who had stayed near the door began their farewells. Iroshi cut them short, pleading too much work and a headache, and the Galician contingent left.

Finally alone, she turned her full attention to Ensi.

"Did Carson's death spook her?"

Probably. And possibly the failure of the last attack. All I really get from her at this distance is anxiety and a strong desire to get away. There is something I cannot quite get to.

"Where is she going?"

Her home world, Lawton.

"All right," she said aloud. "Mark, Erik, contact the racer crew. Have them prepare for departure."

Silently, she said to Ensi, "Contact Mitchell and have another team sent here to finish up the negotiations. They are to bring a full guard. Sheera, Johnson, and Leila will stay and help the new truthsayer. Erik and Mark will come with me."

"I think you should wait until we can get a few more warriors to go with us," Erik spoke up.

I agree with him, Ensi said.

"There isn't time. Walker may not go directly to Lawton. Or she may stop there only a short time, then go on somewhere else. We have to keep track of her. We have to move fast . . ."

Iroshi, you are forgetting someone.

"Who?"

Yail.

She turned to find the young policeman staring at her, clearly unsure of what was happening.

"I'm sorry, my love," she said. "I can't explain all of this right now. I have to leave . . ."

"Who is Walker?" he asked. "The one you have to keep track of."

"A woman named Rhea Walker, who has been behind the attacks."

"How do you know? How do you know she's leaving? I don't understand what's going on."

"I know you don't. I just can't explain right now. We have to move as quickly as possible." She moved closer to him, took his hand in hers. "Can I ask you to help Sheera and the others when they arrive?"

He looked at her a long minute. She hadn't meant to hurt him, but being left out, not knowing what was going on—that would hurt anyone. Especially someone in love.

"Yes," he said at last. "You can ask." He pulled his hand free. "And I will help them. Will I . . ."

He looked around at the others, not wanting to ask the question in front of them.

"Will you see me again?" she asked for him. His eyes met hers. "Yes. I promise. You will see me again."

He stood abruptly.

"I'll leave you to your preparations, then," he said stiffly. "Have them contact me when they are ready for my help."

Iroshi nodded and Yail left.

"The only way he will ever understand is by becoming a member of the Glaive," Iroshi said.

You could not explain otherwise.

She sat, studying the closed door, willing Yail to come back, wanting to tell him everything now. Relationships should not be so complicated. Loving someone should be easy, but it never was. Falling in love was easy. Too damned easy!

Tears stung her eyes, and she shook her head. No time to mourn the loss. Any loss. There was never time.

The cruiser lifted without incident and was soon preparing to enter hyperspace. Rhea Walker did not understand anything about the technology except that it worked. That was all that mattered. Get as far from Bosque as possible. And that Iroshi bitch. Duncan would be proud of everything she had accomplished. She most certainly was.

These Glaive people were the luckiest she had ever seen: two well-planned attacks on the leader, neither successful. There was no reason that she had been able to figure for their failure.

Regardless, the stage had been set for destroying the Glaive anyway. She had turned into quite a rabble-rouser. Felt good having a platform on which to voice the bitter hatred she had nursed so carefully.

What was taking so long? Get into hyperspace, dammit. They had to get far away before the guild racer lifted from the planet. The racer was faster, and if it got too close, the plan would be ruined.

There she felt it, the tingling, first along her scalp, then down her neck, through her body, spreading tendrils teasing her body. Warmth flooded through her, washing away the tingling, announcing they had jumped. Good. The racer could follow but not catch up for some time. By then, it would be too late.

Third time is lucky.

She unstrapped and left the cabin, headed for the bridge. The captain needed to be prodded to make haste in spite of the head start they already had. She had made it halfway down the corridor when the navigator appeared at the far end. They always needed a break after achieving hyperspace. Something about the electrodes implanted in their skulls overheating or some such thing. She shuddered as they passed.

Damn freaks. They should make slaves of all of them.

8

The eyes in the picture stared back in cold appraisal. They had not changed in more than a day, of course. Not since the computer had fed out the print.

Iroshi tossed the picture onto the table. Gods knew that she had looked at it often enough to memorize the features: red hair, like new-minted copper coins; complexion to match, freckles and all. Blue eyes, so light they were almost white. According to the statistics sheet, Mrs. Walker was five feet ten inches tall, weighed one hundred forty-eight pounds, and was thirty-one years old.

She looked a little older in the picture, or maybe that was what Iroshi had expected. A widow should be older, especially when the husband died at age fifty-six. Iroshi set Rhea Walker's picture next to Duncan Walker's on the desktop. He had looked older than his years, too. Maybe dealing in slaves did that to a person.

Hard to believe that people dealt in human lives like that. Even if it was a reestablishment of the old institution of indentured service, it filled her with dread. Every time a new sector of space was opened to colonists, it reappeared, according to the reports gleaned from the computer. The last time was over a hundred years ago.

Sad as it was, a lot of people could only afford to move among the colonies by selling themselves. Passage to new worlds was always so expensive.

Other people always waited behind the scenes, ready to take advantage of the desperate. However, unlike others, the Walkers had taken things one step further.

As far as anyone had determined, they were the only ones trading in slaves from one world to another. The unfortunate individuals were taken from sparsely populated worlds and, occasionally, from ships that broke down.

The worst thing was, not one law agency was working on the problem. That was due, in many locales, to lack of knowledge that the problem even existed, and in part to the fact that, in the overall realm of humanity, it was a very small problem.

Even the Glaive had not pursued it after the initial discovery. Too many other things going on. So why, all of a sudden, was Walker coming after the Glaive? Revenge for the death of her husband? Did she fear that the Glaive would eventually get around to putting her out of business permanently? If that had not already happened.

The reports said that the Donnington Corp. had existed only on paper since its encounter with the Glaive four years ago. That gave an impression of fear. Waiting for the next move may have been too much for the Walkers. He killed himself; she planned revenge.

The whole scenario just seemed too weak. Something was missing.

A knock on the door brought Iroshi out of her reverie. She pushed herself up in the chair.

"Come in."

Captain Ferguson entered the cabin. Not for the first time, she realized that he was getting old. He still stood straight as a ramrod, could hold his own in a fight, and was one of the best spacers in the Glaive. However, he often looked tired, such as at that moment, and one day soon—too soon—she would have to honor his request to retire.

"We're still on track," he reported. "We can catch the Walker ship in a day, maybe less."

"Can you tell where it's headed yet?"

"Looks like the Nelson sector. That *isn't* where their home world is located."

She shook her head. Nothing in the reports had mentioned the Nelson sector. To make matters worse, Ensi could not probe anyone's mind in hyperspace. Too much interference. Plus the fact that distance always made it more difficult when dealing with someone with no trace of telepathy.

The comm buzzed, and Iroshi pressed the button. Garrick's voice came on, tinged with excitement.

"The cruiser is preparing to jump," he said.

Ferguson leapt from the chair and leaned on the desk.

"Prepare to follow," he said.

"Aye, sir."

Iroshi turned the comm off.

"Can we do it safely?" she asked.

"All we can do is try. Coming out of hyperspace, even when you know where you're going, is always a little risky. Coming out when you have no idea . . ." He looked more tired than ever when he looked her square in the eye. "It's your choice. I'll do whatever you want. But we'll have to hurry."

Did they lose the murderers? Or did they jump too soon and risk slamming into a planet—even an asteroid—and killing everyone on board?

"Do it," she said.

Iroshi, I do not think . . .

"I won't lose them, Ensi. Not now."

Ferguson relayed the order over the comm. The exec's voice was slightly strained when he acknowledged the order. The captain hurried out. His place was on the bridge. Should she follow or stay where she was? There was not much she could help with if she followed. But just sitting and waiting was always the hardest thing for her to do.

Let the crew do their work, Ensi said. *That is what they are there for.*

He was right. She would only get in the way, or make them all self-conscious.

Too late, anyway. The ship slowed. Most people said they could not feel it, but she always did. Just before the ship actually jumped out of hyperspace. Then came the tingling along every nerve, particularly the nerve endings in her skin. She crossed her arms and rubbed them. The tingling eased.

Klaxons sounded throughout the ship. A red warning light flashed over the door. The ship swerved abruptly, throwing her off balance.

The racer suddenly bucked, and the sound of an explosion blended with the Klaxons. Iroshi was thrown to the floor.

She got to her knees but the ship bucked again, knocking her over. She stayed down as another explosion rocked them. She managed to get her feet under her and made it out the door. No more explosions, and she got to the bridge in spite of the ship's yawing and shuddering.

"What the hell happened?" she demanded of Ferguson.

"Explosion in the power room and aft," Garrick reported to the captain. "We've lost most of our power and navigation."

"Before that?" she asked.

"We came out of hyperspace too close to a planet," Ferguson answered while keeping a close eye on his crew and the instruments.

"How's Louis?"

"Knocked him off his couch when navigation was hit. Mark is checking him now."

Navigators were always vulnerable when something catastrophic happened to a ship. When hooked up to their controls, they were part of the ship. Iroshi had been there, once. That had been enough.

"Any ships nearby?" the captain asked.

"Can't tell," the exec said.

Ferguson looked at Iroshi. If there were no ships in the area, only one thing could have happened. The racer had been sabotaged. Back on Bosque.

"I'd say we've been a bit lax, Captain," she said as she gripped the back of his command chair. He nodded. "What now?"

"The planet's gravity is pulling us down. We'll have

to see if we can regain enough control to set down somewhere. If we've enough power and navigation. If there's somewhere to set down."

"I'll leave you to your work," she said.

Iroshi turned on her heel and left the bridge. She knew a lot about ships, but Ferguson and his crew were the experts. It was times like these when they earned their reputation as the finest in the fleet. The Glaive fleet was the finest in any sector.

It was their damn security that was lacking! And after everything she had said to Tarek Varia . . .

"Ensi, how in the hell did anyone get near enough to the racer to sabotage it?"

She bounced off one wall, then braced against the other.

Any of a number of ways, he answered quickly. *Also, it could be that no one had to get near. There are numerous remote means of planting a bomb of some sort.*

That was true enough. But for a security organization, theirs was suddenly leaving a lot to be desired.

"Ever get the feeling we've been set up? We find out who's been leading the campaign against us. She leaves immediately after. I decide to pursue. No time to check the ship thoroughly before liftoff."

She slammed open the door to her cabin. Once inside, she slammed it shut. Too bad that didn't make her feel better. She would prefer to slam someone's head. Her own, for starters.

Don't be so hard on yourself, Ensi broke in. *We have all become complacent in the past few years. After all, what have we had to fear since Mushimo's sons were eliminated?*

The comm on her desk buzzed, and she punched the button. Ferguson's face appeared on the small screen.

"Iroshi, Louis is unconscious and won't be able to hook back up and help us land. I'll need Donner to keep the ship stable if we're going to land safely."

Donner was the backup navigator and an excellent pilot. Her talents as a pilot were obviously needed, considering the way the racer was still fighting control.

"Are you suggesting that I take over navigation?" Iroshi asked. Dread settled in her stomach.

"You're the only other person on board who's done it." His own implants had been removed some years before.

"Ensi," she called silently.

I will be with you the whole time.

"All right, Captain. I'll get ready."

She turned the comm off, but she stared into the blank screen at her own reflection for the space of several heartbeats. Navigation could be left vacant for a short time while the others worked at regaining control. That would give her time to do the same. Or give her time to wonder, which could be a bad thing.

Funny, experiencing the link-up with a ship had been something she had wanted for a number of years. Then the last time—the only time—she had entered the navigation network had been a matter of life and death. Like now. Without the necessary electrodes planted in her skull, the only route she could take was to go into revay. To leave her body, concentrate all the energy of her

physical and mental existence. Channel that energy and
consciousness along the ship's consciousness. She had
left navigation behind, traveled along other functions,
first ship's controls, then weapons' controls.

The deaths of that ship, its crew, and Mushimo's
son . . . Remembering brought back the black despera-
tion, their sorrow, their acceptance.

She had not wanted to return to her own body.

After the violence and anguish, she had found peace
of a kind. It washed over her as she remembered.

Iroshi. Iroshi.

Ensi had been calling for some time. He sounded worried. Well, that matched her own feelings exactly.

"There's no other way, Ensi," she said aloud.

I know, but . . .

His confidence had waned. The comm buzzed again.

"We're ready," Ferguson told her.

"It will take a moment," she informed him and prepared to lie down on her bunk.

I am here, Ensi said.

"Yes."

She pressed the light dimmer button until twilight descended in the cabin. The first experience with revay
had been vicarious, seen through Ensi's eyes, listening
to Aicir's voice. Aicir, the spirit ward of the temple on
Rune-Nevas, now bonded with Ronald Hannigan. A
temple of ruins when she first saw it. But that night, centuries before she was even born . . .

Oh, the sadness. All those deaths, the bodies burned,
the loneliness afterward. Sixty-three souls anchored to
the temple yet existing as the air, without form. Until

she came along and accepted Ensi into her mind, her body. At first she thought she was going mad, hearing voices inside her head, seeing people and things that did not exist.

Concentrate. Dive deeper into herself, past memories, past feelings, back to birth agonies. Deeper. Become as the air, yet anchored to the ship and her own body that lay within it.

She flew to the outlets now abandoned by the navigator. Inside, follow the connections, find the coordinates. The ship's skin was cold, metallic, all-embracing. Silence surrounded it. Voices rumbled within. Finding what she needed to guide the ship, finding the planet, bringing the two together. Some sort of magnetic pull from the planet surface. But the ship did not want to cooperate. Signal the pilots, the computers. Coax the right response out of them all.

Closer. They all looked for a good spot to touch down. Too fast! Get out. Navigation is over. Up to the pilots now. Get back just in case.

A weakened section of outer skin crumpled. Air escaped. Power systems shorted out. Hurry! The route is being blocked. Get out!

Sparks pursued along the circuits. She came to a juncture and could not remember which turn to make.

This way, Ensi yelled, but she couldn't find him. *Left!*

She turned. Another short just behind. Explosions everywhere. Route after route cut off. Turn here, there. A bright flash severed the main connection. Behind, fire crackled along the line.

•   •   •

It was taking too long. Waiting, even at this distance, was risky. Still, she had to know. Her hand ached, and she realized she was still gripping the detonator. Rhea Walker set it down on the console next to her chair on the bridge, then looked at the device a long moment. Was it as long-range as she had been told? Had it done the job?

Dammit! How long before they knew?

All of the crew watched their instruments, each eager to yell out if he detected something. They were all fearful, hard-working, and at that moment she could have gladly killed any one of them—maybe all of them—unless someone gave her the word.

They had planned it all carefully, she had to give them credit for that. Bribing a workman at the landing field. Getting the bomb on board the racer, apparently without a Glaive member getting even a hint. Their security was more lax than she would have thought possible. Maybe the Glaive wasn't the threat they had seemed.

Duncan had feared them. Enough to kill himself. But then, he never was terribly brave. Except when facing her.

She shrugged off the memories beginning to unfold. It didn't matter any more what he was like. She was in charge now, and the Donnington Corp. would soon be back in business.

The waiting stretched further. Fifteen minutes had passed from the time she pressed the button. Whether they were dying instantly or not, those on the racer were doomed, Iroshi among them, just as planned. By the time the ship was missed, the exhaust trail would have dispersed. No one knew where the ship had been headed, and the planet—the nearest one when the explosion took out most of their navigation and power—was reportedly unkind to strangers.

She shuddered at the thought. Finding just the right one had taken more than a year alone. All the other details took most of two years.

"They've gone down!" Jellison shouted.

"On the planet?" Walker asked.

"Yes. Except the sensors we sent down haven't picked them up."

"Start jamming," she ordered.

They would take no chances on rescue coming any time soon.

She picked up the detonator and stroked its black metal case. The racer wasn't destroyed, but the next best thing. Any survivors would wish they had never seen that planet. She nodded at the captain and returned to her cabin. She had just opened the door when the comm line twittered. She punched the "on" pad.

"Mrs. Walker," Jellison's voice said. "There's a problem"

"What is it?"

What could possibly be a problem at this stage?

"The racer's emergency beacon is getting through our jamming. I don't know how . . ."

"Find out. The last thing we need is for more Glaivers to show up."

"Yes, ma'am."

The connection clicked off. A moment later she consciously made herself quit tapping her fingernails on the desktop. With all the best equipment available, why was it difficult to do things right?

Half an hour later, Jellison signaled again.

"What is it, Captain?"

"We're still not sure why the jamming didn't work, ma'am. However," he hurried on, "we have discovered that if we leave our jammer off, their signal does not get through. Barron thinks there might be some sort of jamming device down there. When both of them are turned on, they cancel each other out. That might be why our sensors didn't pick them up."

Well, if this was true, it was a stroke of good luck. Let whatever was on the planet keep the racer's signals from getting out, and save on her own ship's energy. Hell, she could stay here almost forever in that case.

What if the jamming from dirtside stopped? It could be an aberration of some kind, something that cycled on and off.

"Keep a watch on their signal," she said. "If it looks like it's getting out again, turn our jammer back on."

"Yes, ma'am."

The comm clicked off again. There had been nothing in the surveys about this phenomenon, but it certainly would be used to best advantage. If she had to take a squad down to search for survivors, it could interfere with her own communications, that was true. But she had the advantage of knowing it existed and knowing its effect. Another plus on her side of the list of strengths and weaknesses.

9

✦✦
✦

"Hurry up!" Ferguson yelled. "Get that cable reconnected."

Like Mitchell, he never had understood all of the talents of Glaive members, although Iroshi had explained them at one time and another. He had not understood any of that, but he did understand how navigators worked. And she was operating in much the same way. Which meant that she was trapped somewhere along the wires and cables that made up the navigation system.

A broken cable or connection was the one thing navigators feared most. That cut them off. Trapped them inside the electronics, and, unless the connections were restored quickly, they could be trapped forever.

He turned away from the work. It would go faster without him looking over their shoulders.

Across the way, Garrick surveyed the damage, fire extinguisher in hand. Erik Greer had already reported that Louis had died. Whether the crash contributed or he had just succumbed to the effects of the earlier explosions was unclear. Mark Greer had been pinned under some equipment and was unconscious.

Ferguson's first concern had been for Iroshi, both her body lying so still in her cabin, and her life's energy rac-

ing through the navigation system. The shock had to
have hit her hardest. She should have exited earlier, but
the ship's reentry had been so unstable.

"That's it," Jarys reported. She stood up and dusted
herself off. "Everything is reconnected."

"Good work," Ferguson said over his shoulder.

At the first word, he had started for Iroshi's cabin to
see if she had successfully returned.

"Ensi. Ensi, where are you?"

No answer. Had they been separated within the system, or did he make it out? She listened, reached out.
There was nothing for her senses. Difficult to believe
that once she had found peace in just such an environ-
ment. Now she felt only fear. Possibly this was what
dying felt like, once the pain was gone.

Yes, she remembered that from Lucas's dying: blackness, emptiness, the sense of floating. It had frightened
her then because it was taking her friend from her. It
frightened her now because it could mean the end of
everything. People, places, responsibilities she had once
been quite willing to abandon for the peace that no
longer enticed her.

She wanted to live!

For gods' sakes, don't panic. Ferguson and the others
are working on getting the lines reconnected. It would
not be long before she could return to her body. Fires,
recent and long past, flashed through her mind. Bodies
consumed until only ash remained.

She wanted to take a deep breath. How else to calm

herself? Memories. The only ones that came were of death or despair.

Remember Crowell. How she loved him still. Her first teacher and lover and friend. His wife, Yumiko, died last year, and he had been devastated at the loss. She had understood more about the Glaive than Mitchell but had wanted nothing to do with its mystical aspects. Think of something else. Mushimo. Dead, too. Mitchell. Back on Rune-Nevas, handling day-to-day problems and tasks. Loving her so unselfishly that she was constantly amazed. Would he be hurt by her liaison with Yail? Mitchell had dallied with other women on rare occasions. It had hurt her. Yes, she was selfish, wanting everything her own way, freedom to do as she pleased, but often unwilling to grant the same freedom to others. Always expecting their loyalty and consideration.

A product of her own personality, or of the way Glaive warriors and truthsayers had come to idolize her?

Both. Even when she didn't know what *everything* might be, she had wanted it all. Struggling on Siebeling as a child, there had never been enough of anything to satisfy her. Always looking for a way out, to find what else there was. For some time, she had thought she had found it all. Until she found Yail.

He was young, relatively inexperienced, and probably as selfish as she was. Yet, he had reawakened feelings she had forgotten about, that she had not even missed. Worse, he had raised up the hungers of her youth. Passion. Love. Excitement. Maybe because of his youth. Maybe because of his passion for her and its newness to both of them. Going back might not be easy.

A flash of energy sparked past her. In another moment, she moved toward the outlet, toward the real world where those problems would have to be sorted out soon.

Iroshi opened her eyes slowly. Too much light, and her head already hurt. Ferguson stood nearby. He reached for the switch and dimmed the lights further.

"Thanks," she said, then wondered if her voice was too low for him to hear.

"You're welcome," he said.

One mystery solved.

"The ship?"

"Damaged," he said. "We're checking it out now. You look exhausted."

"Yeah. I'd better . . ." She tried to sit up, but movement only made her head hurt worse.

"Not now. We're taking care of what we can. Get a little sleep. We'll need you later."

She settled back down. He was right; she could hardly keep her eyes open. They would need her later.

The first thing she did when she woke two hours later was tour the ship. When Ferguson said "damaged," he had understated the situation a little. Two sections could not even be lived in on the ground, much less in airless space. The power plant was half gone, the other half usable only if you wanted to take a chance with what remained of your life. The computer stuttered, when they could keep it on-line more than two minutes, and the backup system would not boot up. Navigation worked okay, since that was the first thing repaired, except the computer wouldn't stay up long enough to get it on-line anymore.

With the computer out, the comm system would not work, not that the system itself had survived unscathed. Worse yet, none of the companions had been able to reach anyone off-planet.

And on and on. The ship was repairable, yes. But without a fully equipped facility? Yeah, right! Everyone kept trying to think positively, but even she knew the job would take days, maybe weeks.

The best chance of rescue lay in the hands of those left behind. Mitchell would soon be alerted on Rune-Nevas, not by any normal communication but by the lack of *any* communication.

Ensi had tried over and over to contact another companion on the home world, but to no avail. Nor could he reach any other location, although he, Savron, and Garon were able to talk to each other as long as they stayed fairly close together. The same was true of personal comm links for the crew and hosts. There seemed to be some sort of jamming signal. However, no contact was almost as good as contact, since that would create concern in time, she reminded herself. The only thing was, lack of communication did not tell anyone where they were.

In the other direction, Yail and the others had a better idea of where the racer was headed. However, without the exact coordinates . . . Well, space was rather large.

"Well planned," she muttered.

"What?" Ferguson said.

"I was just thinking how well planned this whole thing was."

"True," he said. "Exiting hyperspace suddenly—the odds of our running into a solid object were pretty great. The bomb going off at just the right time to disable maneuvering. And, since it all happened right out of hyperspace, not much chance of our being traced here."

They had completed the circuit through the ship and were back at her cabin. They stepped inside, she sat in her usual chair at the desk, and the captain sat in the chair opposite.

"Once we get the computers on-line, the first thing we need to determine is where we are," Iroshi said. "I think that should be our first priority."

"Agreed," Ferguson said. "Only two men can work on the computers at a time, though. In the meantime, we had better get the ship sealed as much as we can. The atmosphere here is mostly nitrogen and oxygen, but without the sensors working properly we can't be sure what else there may be."

They started to prioritize repairs and inventories. Her spirits ebbed the further along they got. Food and water were all right for four or five days, but they would need the automatic systems back up by then, or else they would start getting both hungry and thirsty. The ship looked bad enough to depress even the greatest optimist. An inventory of the rest of the problems did not help.

After half an hour, a course of action was planned for repairs and Ferguson left her cabin. So far he had worked tirelessly, but he looked too tired. She had or-

dered him to get some sleep when he started to argue at her *suggestion*. He was no good to them if he collapsed.

"Well, Ensi, what do you think?"

We are in trouble. Not only because of the things you and the captain discussed. This damping field, or whatever it is that keeps me from reaching anyone off this planet, seems to originate right here on-planet. For a short while, we were able to get signals out, although I was sure the damper was operating. It was almost as if something had created a null field.

Looked like someone was determined to isolate them.

"Any ideas yet on where the damper might be?"

None. It is definitely artificial. You or Erik should take a walkabout to give a companion an opportunity to analyze, send data back, so we can determine how extensive it is. We can work on a direction, he said, meaning him and the other companions.

"It's a big planet. What do you expect anyone to find on foot?"

The source of the field must be near. Its electrical and magnetic influence may be the reason we landed in this area.

So it had not been her imagination.

"And I thought it was my wonderful work as navigator. I'll go a little later . . ."

On second thought, I would rather one of the brothers went so I can study . . .

"You don't want me risking myself."

We have no idea what may be out there.

"Why risk both of their lives? Mark is already injured and . . ."

You cannot be all things, Iroshi. Noble gestures are often only that. Besides, that is what Erik and Mark get paid for.

"Getting cynical on me?"

As for the damper, he continued, ignoring her question, *there is little doubt that Walker is around somewhere. This entire incident being her idea, she no doubt would hang around to ensure that her efforts were not wasted. She—rather, her ship—could be the source. We must remain on our guard at all times.*

"But you said there was a moment when the damper was nullified."

I know. That is what has led us to believe there may be two sources at work here. Whether both are Walker's . . .

They left speculation along those lines for later. After a little more general planning, Iroshi found Erik and told him what they needed him to do beginning the next morning. He hesitated a moment, clearly considering his responsibility to protect her, and possibly his brother's condition, but he uttered no protest.

Sleep did not come easily that night. No matter how she tried to justify her decision, Louis's death and Mark's injury haunted her. Ensi tried his best to make her see logic and quit blaming herself. However, after two hours of tossing on the bunk, she got up. Standing in the middle of the cabin, she considered practicing, but her body ached from the physical work. Meditation, then.

She lit a candle, placed it on the floor, and sat down with it in front of her. The flame danced, holding her attention, erasing all other thoughts. Settle in. Think of nothing. Clear the mind.

Emptiness. Warm darkness that caressed, protected. Floating on a breeze that enveloped, smelled sweet like summer flowers. Racing through a landscape on all fours, panting, eager. Hunger lying heavy in the stomach. Sniffing the air. Food just ahead. Behind, others, keeping pace, knowing what to do.

Dodging tall, slender trees and reddish boulders. Over a fallen tree. Foot pads pounding after as the others jumped the tree in succession. Food getting nearer. It could smell the enemy coming, and it was confused. Keep it confused. Tell it that danger came from the opposite direction.

Strategy, unplanned, a matter of instinct. Confuse the instincts of the prey.

There. A flash of tan as prey ran across their path. Faster. Intercept. There, straight ahead. Leap! Talons ripping the shoulder and back. Bite the back of the neck. A cry of terror. Falling. Hold on. The others grabbing the throat, the nose. One landed on the haunches, holding down the thrashing food.

Blood, warm and sweet, seeping between the teeth. Another cry, muffled, weaker.

Iroshi. Come out of it.

A voice in the distance.

Fons Ensi Fae Goron, it said.

Joy fell away as Ensi shouted his full name, the key to unlocking her mind. Retching, Iroshi leapt to her feet and lunged for the bathroom. Even vomiting did not erase the taste of blood from her mouth. She rinsed with mouthwash and chewed some mint that she kept in her toiletries. Better. Wiping the tears from her eyes, she stumbled to her bunk.

"What was that, Ensi?"

Carnivores. Native to this planet. They are animals, yet . . . They are telepathic.

She got up and extinguished the candle, put it on the desk, and returned to the bunk.

They use their minds to confuse their prey . . .

"I got that, thank you. Can they do the same to us? Confuse us, I mean. Why were their thought projections so strong? They were so far away."

They may confuse those who have telepathic abilities. As for the others, I have no way of knowing yet. As for the strength of their projections . . .

He said nothing further. He was as shaken by the incident as she was. More tired than ever, Iroshi at last dropped into sleep in the early hours of morning. She woke at the sound of pounding and drilling, feeling nauseated yet sated by the night's hunt.

Iroshi gave Erik one of the pistols from the arms locker, and watched him exit through the hatch. The immediate area had already been checked at Ferguson's orders, but they knew nothing about this world. Real danger might look as harmless as those trees did. Erik disappeared among the plants that grew to towering heights on one side of the clearing in which the ship sat. His direction had been set by the companions based on where the damping signal seemed to originate.

She stood there for several minutes. Ensi retreated in

order to maintain constant contact with Garon, Erik's companion. A sense of dread washed through her, and she shivered convulsively. Must be the emptiness that came when Ensi withdrew. Yet . . . an ominous quality shadowed the landscape.

The trees were not really trees. The ground cover was not grass. The colors were dark, the shapes vaguely wrong. They were *almost* right. Maybe that was what made the hair rise on the back of her neck: everything was a caricature of what she was accustomed to. Using familiar names did not create a familiarity with the growths themselves. Still, they were the best words they knew.

With another glance around, she went down the ramp. At the end she checked the surroundings again. Nothing moved except twigs and blades of grass in a slight breeze. Unlike Erik, who had just stalked away, she stepped onto the ground tentatively. After all, he had Garon checking all around while Ensi, concentrating on the two of them, left her unprotected. Maybe she had come to depend on Ensi's keeping watch a little too much.

The dark grey-green mat crackled under her boots like dried grass. She stopped at the edge of the woods, reached toward one of the tree trunks. She pulled back. There were stories from other worlds of acid plants and leaves with razor-sharp edges.

Close up, the trees looked less like trees but, by the same token, less ominous, as if they had given up their pretense. She leaned close to one of the towering plants. The outer layer of the trunk was a glossy sheath, streaked with bright colors—red, orange, yellow—and darker browns and greys. She leaned back to see the top. That close to the base the tree seemed even taller than from a distance; it was probably a hundred and fifty feet high at least, with a circumference of ten feet or less. The breeze gusted, the trunk swayed, and she jumped back.

It had seemed alive. Dancing, almost.

Imagination!

She headed back to the racer, turning at the end of the ramp. The trees and grasses swayed in the wind. The rustling sound was crisper than normal, at least normal for Rune-Nevas, or Earth even. Yes, imagination.

It was time to get inside, see where she could help with repairs. Keeping busy was important for them all, not only in their efforts to get off-planet, but also to keep them from thinking too much. About whether or not they *would* get off. About what brought them to this state of affairs. About Walker, whether long gone or hovering overhead, exultant at escaping, at besting the Glaive. About Louis, who may have died because of the decision to follow out of hyperspace at the wrong time.

Maybe the wrong time. If the bomb had gone off while they were in hyperspace, their chances of surviving the explosion might have been less. Ferguson had mentioned that. She knew the danger of such events.

Work. That was what she needed.

Keep straight through that opening ahead, Garon instructed.

Erik had stopped to take in the surroundings a moment. The forest—if it could be called that—seemed to go on forever in all directions. This part of the world, at least, was made gloomy by the thick growth. The feeling of oppression did not help.

Back at the racer, the oppression had been slight, just a little feeling of being closed in. That feeling had grown the farther from the ship he went. He resumed walking, heading in the direction that Garon indicated, but his footsteps became reluctant.

Another ten minutes, and the feeling grew to one of near total isolation. He tried the comm, but it remained silent.

"Garon, can you still contact Ensi?"

A little. It becomes more difficult the farther we go. The effects of the damping field are stronger.

Erik rounded a bend in the path and stopped short. Ahead, a great hill rose from the forest, trees growing more thinly right up to its base. Perched on the sides and the top of the hill were ruins of an ancient settlement. From what he could see, a large settlement, particularly if the ruins lay as thickly on every side of the hill as they did on this side.

"Do you think the source of the damping field is in there somewhere?"

Quite possibly. The only way to know is to search the city.

"Yeah. Do you really want to do this?"

After a long pause, Garon answered, *No.*

"Let's get it over with."

The ruins of a rock wall surrounded the base of the hill, with several gates giving passage through. The wall had been so lowered by weather, and possibly other forces, that he could easily climb over it anywhere along its length. Even so, he chose to enter by one of the gates. Erik passed into the city and halfway up the hill along a broad avenue running from top to bottom. He turned and looked back the way he had come. After what must have been centuries of decay, the forest had not encroached within the encircling walls, as if someone still tended to the perimeter.

From the top, where he got a broader view, the impression that someone had worked to keep the forest back was even stronger. Inside the useless walls, not one building boasted a complete roof, nor more than a few feet of rock wall.

The hilltop was flat and broad, more like a mesa, where all the vertical avenues converged like the spokes of a wheel. Horizontal roads circled at intervals along the sides and around the top. He walked this elevated perimeter along another fallen wall, then worked his way to the imposing center building, from which he found it difficult to take his eyes.

The central rotunda still possessed nearly half of its domed roof. Wings extended from each side and from the back. On closer inspection, the walls were more complete than they had at first seemed.

"We've seen very little alive yet," Erik said to Garon.

A few small animals. Like small rodents. They are shy, but not as afraid as one might think. I wonder if this city might not be a sanctuary to them.

"You mean they live on this hill in relative safety from predators?"

An impression only, but yes. Have you noticed that the feeling of enclosure has changed since we entered its precincts?

"Yes."

I can no longer hear Ensi, and he does not answer me.

"That means the damping mechanism is here."

He turned to gaze at the surrounding buildings a moment. Every one had been constructed of grey stone—at least, grey now—that probably came from some distance away. On the trek to the site, he had passed through thick forest without one sign of a quarry. Even after centuries, perhaps a thousand years, there should be evidence of outcroppings of stone if they existed, but there had been none.

"Let's look inside," he said and turned toward the central building.

From the marks on the stone frame, an immense single door had once covered the entry, of what material no trace could be seen. Within the rotunda, Erik found himself under the central dome. Above, the half-roof let in shafts of sunlight that lit all but the most recessed corners. Smaller doorways, spaced along either side, yawned greyly, uninviting at best. Directly opposite the main entrance ran a hallway, darkening a few feet inward until blackness shrouded its end.

Dirt and dust muffled his footsteps as he moved warily from one door opening to another. An occasional seedling poked through the dirt among shards of stone and masonry, growing from seeds probably borne on the wind.

The walls inside had been covered with some sort of plaster that had then been carved and painted with figures that were still discernible. Most of the figures to the left were of stars and constellations.

"Maybe this was an observatory."

Or possibly a university.

Nearer the central passageway, the carvings changed from simple charts to some sort of inscriptions. Although it was clearly writing of some type, Erik could make nothing of them. However, Garon became more excited than the host had ever felt him. Within, the companion kept murmuring, *Runes. Runes.*

10

✦✦
✦

Iroshi shook her head, trying to concentrate on connections for the food replicator. Two nights and three days on this godforsaken planet—if you counted the day of the crash as one day. Except for the fact that she had no appetite, the days were not too hard for her to endure. It was the nights that had become a misery.

Erik walked past; dark circles showed under his eyes, too. Mark was not recovering from his injuries the way he should have been. Since the first night, he had refused any food. In his weakened condition, he would not last much longer without eating something. Between worrying about his brother and being tormented by the nightly excursions, Erik was suffering even more than she was.

She had tried to talk to Mark, find out for sure that he was having the same dreams, the same visitations each night. However, he was delirious and said nothing rational. He did mutter often, but only a few words were intelligible: "hunt," "kill," and "blood" were the most telling. Clearly, the same experiences tormented him that she and Erik were experiencing. The two of them had talked about it; one result was agreement on where the dreams came from. No solution to the problem occurred to either.

Nor could any of the companions help. The thought projections from the carnivores seemed to be slowly driving Ensi, Savron, and Garon slightly mad. Try as they might, they could not come up with any way to keep away the thoughts. Building a wall of mental blocks had always worked against unwanted projections, but these animals were so primitive, their thoughts so base, there seemed to be no way to keep them from intruding.

Yet they were not entirely thoughts. Instinct and emotion drove these creatures. Hunger forced them to hunt each night. Several of them in the pack. How many, she had not been able to tell. It was always the leader's eyes that she saw through, his mind that touched hers. He never looked at his companions closely during the period of contact. Nor could she get a clear sense of his appearance.

He was four-legged, with great hearing and night vision. Impossible to tell if he saw in color, since there was so little light. Although the moon was bright, so far it had risen after the animals had sated themselves on the night's kill.

Sated. That feeling pervaded her being each morning when she woke. Between that and the feeling of nausea at having eaten such fresh raw meat and drunk blood . . . But she had not done that. Still, his pleasure at the feast flooded both body and mind, and the very thought of food made her sick. Neither she nor Erik could continue without food or sleep very long. However, Mark was the one in real danger. How much longer could he hang on in his weakened condition?

"Ensi."

He didn't answer. It was becoming difficult to sense his presence, and when he didn't answer, which was happening more often, panic settled in her empty stomach.

"Ensi, please answer."

I am here.

He sounded tired. That was frightening. She swallowed and took a deep breath, trying to calm herself.

"I think we should start working at night and sleeping during the day."

The thoughts would still come. You would be distracted from anything you were working on, including standing guard.

"It would still be better for us. It would have to be."

Try it if you must.

She could not stand his air of resignation. It was totally out of character and, in a way, she could not understand it. He did not have a body to get worn out. Maybe it was simply that his mind was taking the full brunt of the thoughts.

"Any luck coming up with some way to block them?"

No. We are still working on it. Their brains operate on such a basic level that we cannot find the right combination.

"What about the mind vampire? Was there anything in that experience that could help?"

Not really. That was a thinking being. Very sophisti-

*cated, even though single-minded. With these animals,
we are encountering instinct and basic drives: hunger,
survival. Things that we all take for granted.*

*You must send Erik back to the ruined city. We are
certain that an answer lies there. The runes . . .*

Even she had recognized them: rune inscriptions very
much like the ones found on Rune-Nevas in all of the
ruins there. Ensi had taught her to read them so she
could convince people that she had found the temple
treasures through these inscriptions and texts discovered in the temple. Through them, too, she had learned
more of the history of the people who had lived on that
world, adding that knowledge to the lessons Ensi had
taught.

From the small sample from the domed building,
they had detected differences, of course, in the words
and meanings. Ensi had insisted on several occasions
that Erik be sent back so the companions could study
the inscriptions, determine for certain if there was a
connection between the extinct civilization that had
lived here and his own on Rune-Nevas. She had been
reluctant to do so, particularly after discovering the carnivores. Just making the trip could be dangerous. Erik
was reluctant himself, since it would mean leaving his
brother.

Then there was the change in the damping effect on
the hill that Erik had described. It could mean that the
invasion of their minds by the carnivores might be
blocked if they stayed within the supposed sanctuary.
On the other hand, it was possible that the change in the
effect would be harmful somehow. If the effects were

not harmful, should they all move into the ruins? Work on the ship during the day, sleep in the ruins at night. How would that affect their chances of being rescued? Would someone come, think everyone was dead because they couldn't contact them, and leave without checking, or even knowing about, the ancient city?

This was ridiculous! The immediate consideration was surviving. Their best chance was probably to stay in the ruins, but she wanted to see them first.

She squeezed her eyes shut against a wave of nausea. When it passed, she called Ensi and, when he responded, told him that she was going to the ruins herself.

"Don't start harping on not endangering myself. Moving everyone there might be our best hope for survival, but I can't make that decision without seeing what's there. I want to go before dark today. Once the sun goes down, I'll be able to tell if there's protection from the carnivores' thoughts, and see if there's any kind of danger within its precincts. From what Erik described, there are a few buildings that would be comfortable. Sounded like the central building is the best bet."

Ensi maintained a stony silence, and she began feeling like she was babbling to fill the void.

"I'll take Erik with me. Neither of us is much good here as far as detecting approaching danger. Not with this damping effect. So our absences will have little effect either way."

All right. I would like to feel the spirit of the place more closely.

"Spirit? Gods, I hope there are no ghosts in these ruins."

She went looking for Ferguson to discuss the trip. Like Ensi, he feared for her safety but had no choice but to go along with her plan.

He changed the work schedule, and she and Erik were set to leave one hour before sundown. That would get them inside the walls at about the time the carnivores began waking. Next she went looking for Erik. Garrick said he was on a break, and that meant one thing: he was with Mark in the infirmary. Probably trying to get him to eat.

As she approached, voices and the sounds of scuffling were very loud.

"Hold him!" Erik shouted.

Someone barked like a dog, a sound that sent chills up her spine. She rushed into chaos. Erik and Jarys were trying to hold Mark on the bunk. Mark thrashed around, fighting them as hard as he could. Jarys kept trying to fasten restraining straps to the bunk, but Mark managed to keep pushing her away.

Iroshi wrapped her left arm around his flailing ankles, pressing the feet to the blanket. Jarys fastened a strap on the far side, then the near side, then pulled it taut across his shins. Iroshi struggled to get her arm from underneath. Free, she pressed with both hands on Mark's knees. Erik cried out as his brother scratched his cheek but regained his hold on Mark's arms. Jarys got a strap over the thighs.

Erik pulled the flailing arms over Mark's head. Iroshi pressed her body over the brother's chest. Jarys fastened straps over the waist, then over the chest after Iroshi moved down the sweaty body. It took both Iroshi and Erik to get the left arm down by the side so it could be pinioned without breaking it. Then they maneuvered the right arm.

Mark now interspersed the barking with howling, a sound both eerie and primitive. He bounced his head up and down, his fingers grasping at air. Erik and Jarys caught his head in a downward motion, pressed it against the mattress while Jarys secured it.

The three backed away, each breathing hard. Through veiled eyes and sideways glances, they surveyed their handiwork. Mark was strapped to the bunk, but his struggles had not ceased. The bunk bounced up and down and side to side.

"We'll have to fasten it against the wall," Jarys said.

Iroshi and Erik pushed it against the wall; then Jarys got pins out of a drawer. From another drawer, she got a power tool. When she approached the bunk Iroshi turned her back against it and pushed to keep it flush against the wall. Jarys's scream made her turn back.

Mark had clamped his teeth on Jarys's upper arm as she leaned over him. Off balance, she could not extricate herself. Erik dove for the bunk and pressed his thumbs on Mark's jaws, forcing them apart. Iroshi pulled Jarys away, supporting her as Jarys's knees buckled slightly.

Cursing fluently, Erik finished fastening the bunk to the wall while Iroshi tended Jarys's wound.

"Damn, look at all that blood," Jarys said through clenched teeth. "I'm going to have a scar for sure."

"Think of it as one of the more unusual battle scars in the Glaive," Iroshi said.

The medic grinned.

"Give Mark a sedative or whatever will quiet him down," Iroshi said.

"With his fever and weakened condition, that could be dangerous," Jarys said.

"Any more dangerous than his breaking that bunk loose? We've got to keep him from harming himself."

Jarys agreed.

"Come on," Iroshi said to Erik, and started herding him out of the room. When she looked back one last time, the medic was surveying the mess on the floor. Mark had broken every piece of equipment that had been set up to rehydrate and feed him, and everything else he'd gotten his hands on.

She guided Erik to the galley, made him sit down, drew him a cup of hot tea, and fixed one for herself. She sat down across from him, and they sat in silence for several minutes.

Mark's actions had been totally unexpected. There had been no hint of thoughts from the carnivores as far as she was concerned. So . . . Was Mark more sensitive to their slightest thought because of his weakened condition? Or, perhaps more likely, had he been dreaming, reliving the experiences of the night before?

"I'm afraid he's going to die," Erik said suddenly. "I don't know how much more of this *I* can stand, and I'm not injured or feverish, or . . ."

He took a quick gulp of the tea.

"I talked to the captain," Iroshi said. "You and I are

going to check out the ruins. See if we might be able to stay there. If that damping effect blocks the carnivores' thoughts within those walls, we'll all be better off. Ferguson's making up the new work schedule now. We should get a few hours of sleep before we leave."

"Will it help the nights if we sleep there?"

"I hope so."

Erik nodded. "Maybe."

They concentrated on drinking their tea. Until now, they had not discussed many details about what was happening in the visions. Mostly, they had confirmed that they were both experiencing the carnivores' hunting and feeding in rather vague terms. Would it help if they talked about what they saw and felt?

"Where are you in the pack?"

His head jerked up, a look of surprise on his face. The look was replaced by one of disgust. Clearly, he did not want to talk about it, but suddenly she felt compelled to.

"I'm in the lead," she said. "I'm the first one to leap. I taste the first blood . . ."

Erik jumped to his feet.

"I'm none of them," he shouted. "They are not me . . ."

"Which one?" she asked quietly.

They stared at each other, she waiting for his reply, he poised for flight. Another moment and he slumped, looked defeated.

"I'm at the back of the pack," he said in a low voice. "I watch the leader as much as I watch the prey. I think he's wanting to become the leader."

He had switched from "I" to "he" deliberately, emphasizing the latter. She exhaled loudly and hit the tabletop with both fists.

"Keep thinking that," she said. "It's them. We are not doing the killing. Or the feeding. Hold onto your own being."

He looked surprised again, and she tried to relax and speak in a more normal voice.

"I'm getting worried about the companions. This has been even harder on them."

"I just keep hoping they can find some way to block the transference," he said. "I never expected something like this."

"No one did. No one ever expected to find beasts that were telepathic. Even with people we usually find individuals, not whole societies, with this ability."

"Except on Rune-Nevas."

"Yeah, except there. But the priest-warriors were unique within their own society. And their telepathic abilities were enhanced when they left their bodies."

"It . . . It's getting stronger," he said, as if he had not heard. "The feeling of being it. Of wanting to taste . . ."

"Go on and get some sleep," she said when he left the thought unfinished. "I'm on my way, too."

He nodded and stood up.

"We'll do everything we can for Mark," she said. Erik nodded again and left the galley.

However much that might be, she thought. If they did not soon get some relief, all three of them might not make it. Her stomach rumbled and she considered looking for a piece of fruit, something light, but her throat tightened. Maybe tomorrow.

She put the cups in the processor and headed for her cabin. Once inside, she was almost asleep before her head hit the pillow.

11

✦

Twilight turned the trees into even more ominous shapes than in daylight. A steady breeze kept them moving, not swaying as familiar trees did, but jerking, dancing, circling the clearing where the racer lay dead.

Iroshi rubbed her eyes. In spite of the weirdness of the trees, the scheme seemed to be working pretty well. She had actually slept for a few hours, although not totally undisturbed. Erik had said the same. The beasts slept during the day and dreamed. Their dreams were not as exhausting as the nightly hunts—running, leaping, bringing down prey—but were still disturbing. Dreams broken by spells of comparative quiet.

None of the dreams, nor the hunting projections, had prepared her for . . . It had come as a strange physical sensation. The pack leader, lying on its side, raised its head, looked toward its hindquarters. Its rear legs were slightly parted. Two pups pressed against her, nursing.

The leader was a female. Was that why her thoughts tormented Iroshi, rather than another pack member's? And, since the leader would be more forceful, maybe even more creative, she would project more forcefully.

But Erik's contact? A male. Wanting to be the leader? Yes, he stared at the leader from the back of the pack-when they ran. He was more intent on her than on the prey. And Mark's tormentor? Actually, there was no reason he might not be receiving the same projections as Erik. Especially if it was possible that female matched to female and male to male.

Erik walked up at that moment, releasing her from endless speculation. He shifted the rifle from one arm to the other as he sat down beside her.

He had been more upset about the delayed trip to the ruins than she had, even though Ensi had assured both of them that Mark would be all right for another few days. However, once Erik accepted that moving to the ruins might be the one thing that would save his brother, he had wanted to act as quickly as possible.

Ensi had explained that the three companions felt close to a breakthrough in communication and wanted to concentrate on that effort. In spite of her feelings that it was a lost cause, Iroshi had agreed to give them the time. Meantime, she and Erik had gotten as much sleep as they could in preparation for the night's work: guarding the site and effecting a few minor repairs.

Just in case they became unable to maintain their guard, she had arranged for members of the crew to check on them periodically throughout the night. Not an ideal situation but, until they knew how rearranging the schedules would work, it was the best they could do.

"I thought I'd take a break and check on Mark," Erik said at last. "Switching night and day seems to have helped you and me, but . . ."

He shrugged. Mark had no respite, or at least not enough in his weakened condition. That must be another part of the equation. The human minds had to be at rest or unguarded . . .

Her vision blurred, and now familiar feelings grabbed her.

"They're hunting," she said.

"I know," Erik said breathlessly.

Although she was seated, the feeling of being off balance brought her to all fours. She tried to keep her eyes open, concentrate on the ship's surroundings, but the other scenes rushed between.

"Ensi," she called aloud. "I need you."

No answer. He had been remote all day; their contact had been so infrequent that she had felt alone even in sleep. Or, would have if the other dreams had not kept her entertained off and on.

Can't stay on the ground. Get someone else out here. She and Erik were impotent at that point. She tried to sit up at the very moment the beast leapt over a fallen tree. Dizziness from conflicting motions kept her down. This was not right. The two of them were wide awake, more in control. Yet the sensations were stronger than ever.

"Erik, we have to get help," she whispered.

The brother moaned. He still sat upright. Neither of them moved.

What if the carnivores were racing toward the ship? The two of them were useless as guards at that moment. Concentrate on building the barrier. Brick by brick. Maybe it would help just enough. Sweat broke out on her forehead. She struggled, but nothing worked.

I have wakened Captain Ferguson, Ensi informed her suddenly. Then he was gone again.

The struggle stopped. The hunt—it was the hunt that mattered.

"Iroshi! Iroshi!"

Hands grasped her shoulders, shook her. Raised her to sit up. A dream.

There! Straight ahead. A lumbering animal. Favorite food. Mouth watering. Whining behind from the young one. A more experienced animal nipped him on the flank, and he quieted. The prey looked up. Fear filled the air. Leap. Clamp down on the neck. Hold on while the others grabbed wherever they could and pulled it down. She landed hard on her side, the animal almost pinning her to the ground. A short struggle, and she was back on her feet. She opened her jaws, releasing her hold, licked her lips. Sweet blood. Chase the others back. Tear at the stomach, release the sweetest parts.

Hands held her down, and she struggled against them. Another dream, a nightmare. She must be sated before the rest could eat their fill.

The long-distance transmission flickered, and Jiron Yail's visage blinked out and in. Concern made his jaw muscle jump and his mouth tighten into a thin line. He was not a member of the Glaive, so his concern was based on something other than Glaive loyalty. He had said that he had acted as liaison for Iroshi while she was on Bosque. Was that all?

Mitchell mentally shook off the thought. This was hardly the time to suddenly find himself jealous of one of Iroshi's romantic liaisons. There had never been time before, and there certainly was none now.

Iroshi's racer had lifted from Yail's world four days earlier, destination unknown except that it was following a private cruiser. Yail had personally confirmed the logged departure and crew and passengers on board. One day—give or take a few hours—after departure, both the racer and the cruiser disappeared from all tracking. Not entirely surprising, since ships could not be tracked while in hyperspace. However, Glaive ships rarely stayed out of contact more than five hours at a time. Jumps almost never lasted even that long.

Even so, no one panicked for seven hours after jump was initiated. The time in hyperspace sometimes played weird tricks on comm systems, even navigation systems, and losing contact for a short time was not unusual. However, with redundant systems installed on all ships, losing them for more than a day was cause for worry.

The view screen flickered again, then cleared. Improvements over the past decade or so notwithstanding, communications were susceptible to too many outside influences. Yail's frustration at the difficulties had deepened the existing creases in his forehead and around his mouth.

"Still no word," he repeated. "One of our small traders has been requisitioned, and we'll be taking off within the hour. There should be some energy traces. Since they commed back their jump window before contact was lost, we hope there will be enough to indicate their jump exit."

"What's taken so long?" Mitchell asked. He had initiated a search pattern for all likely sectors two days earlier. Unfortunately, Glaive ships were badly scattered.

"Events sometimes move slowly in Galicia," the younger man said. "Since our officials have been reluctant to commit to supporting the Glaive in this matter . . ."

"It's their matter, too. None of this would have happened if we hadn't sent a representative to help you."

"I know, Mitchell. I know. Except the Council has convinced itself that none of this would have happened if the Glaive had not been here."

"That may be true, but . . ." Mitchell sighed. The young policeman had probably been the driving force behind the Galician's sending even this one ship. "This is doing no one any good. If we have to, we'll sort out blame after the racer has been found. Are Sheera, Johnson, and Leila prepared to go with you?"

"Yes. The doctors thought Leila should stay in their care a little longer, but she insists on going. I don't think it will be a problem for her. Mostly what she needs now is rest. I hardly think she'll get much of that either way, but the chances are better if she isn't back here wondering what's going on."

Mitchell nodded. Devotion within the Glaive was one thing they could count on. Too bad security was not another. Dammit, he had worried on more than one occasion that procedures were becoming lax. He should have spoken up, but he always felt that the members knew more than he did. Which was true about some things. However, in the future he would voice any concerns he might have.

"I'm leaving Rune-Nevas in a couple of hours," he said. "As we agreed, I'll head toward Bosque, checking on the way. If we find nothing, we'll rendezvous in sector 139 as planned."

Yail nodded. "Hopefully, one of us will have found some trace by then."

"Good luck."

Mitchell switched off.

There was so much to do to get ready. He had to . . .

What did he have to do? Not much, really. The ship's crew was taking care of preparing the ship. Aides were packing for him. Gregory, his backup, had been briefed last night and was already managing things. Fact was, he needed something to do.

Iroshi and Yail had been lovers. That much he was sure of. The policeman was so damned young. Definitely not the first man to catch her attention. And, Mitchell admitted to himself, he had not been the picture of fidelity either. There was the time he went to Earth to set up the training program in Crowell's dojo. And when he went to Marcus IV—he could not remember why he was there but he did remember Felicia. Both of those encounters were long ago. He would never have had an affair with someone on Rune-Nevas, and he rarely traveled off-world.

How many lovers had she had in their twenty-three years together? Not as many as there were opportunities. But enough to . . . He had started to use the word "bother," but he had never been bothered by them. Until now. Yail was just so damned young.

Better shake it off. There was work to be done. He simply could not sit and wait any longer.

Iroshi had been in danger before. More times than he liked to remember. This was the first time that he was not just worried, he was fearful. Before, the fact that she was good at taking care of herself bolstered his belief that everything would be all right. Not this time. She was in very real danger.

He shook his head and stood. Next thing he knew, he would be reading minds, too. That was not something he had ever wanted.

Yail looked around his cabin on board the trader ship. He had understood Mitchell's frustration all too well. His own frustration had been equal. That was one of the problems with living on a backward world: no one ever saw the larger picture and quite often people would not take responsibility for their actions.

Lord, he wanted to get away from Bosque; leaving Galicia simply was not enough. Aulda offered little respite from provincial thinking. The Glaive was the place to be. Travel from world to world, always learning new things, meeting new people. Sure, it probably became difficult at times, but no price was too big.

When he'd heard that Iroshi was coming to Galicia herself, his only thought had been to meet her somehow. He had seen becoming her lover as one way to get what he wanted. Becoming her friend was another. Convincing her that he was good at his profession was the most important.

Falling in love was never part of the plan.

She was everything he admired in a woman: strong-willed, powerfully situated, even rash to a point. That she was bonded to another man had not mattered at first. After all, it was only an attempt to further his ambitions through a liaison with a woman he was attracted to. At first.

He had never been in love before. The strength of his feelings was surprising.

Relationships were not supposed to be complicated. In Galicia, it was only marriage arrangements that were complicated. Actually, this new relationship was complicated only by Iroshi's disappearance. She had not seemed the least bit reluctant to get involved. Well, that wasn't entirely true. The difference in their ages had bothered her and even he had worried that it might make romancing her difficult; until he met her. Looking into those green eyes was what undid him. Maybe she didn't look or act her age because she was born on another world, or because she traveled so much.

That's what he wanted—to travel. To see distant worlds. He no longer thought of them as exotic; that only meant they were different, anyway. No use in setting himself up for disappointment.

The captain announced the jump into hyperspace. As soon as the jump was made, Yail planned to head for the bridge. He and Sheera would work directly with the captain in trying to find the energy trail that would lead to the missing racer.

Please let Iroshi be all right.

He braced himself in the chair, waiting for the jump

to begin. He had only experienced hyperspace once before, when his parents had sent him on a pleasure trip in an attempt to sway him from the decision to become a policeman. It hadn't worked, of course. But that trip had been like an appetizer, a tease, making him want more.

His hands and feet began tingling. It was just as he remembered.

12

✦

Early morning sunlight turned the fog a light grey. It might be hours before the fog would burn off. It might be hours before Iroshi would feel strong enough to make the trek to the ruins. Even now, when her own thoughts were all that filled her head, she could not sleep. Every time she closed her eyes, excitement raced through her body, the taste filled her mouth.

Erik was asleep, driven by exhaustion. Mark was considerably weaker. They might be well advised to move him and themselves to the ruins *without* checking out the effects of the damping field that *might* be centered in the ruins.

Might. Maybe. Perhaps.

Only guesses about everything. If only she had insisted on making the trip last night. Ensi wished the same thing. The effect of the hunt on him had been devastating. While the chase was in progress, he had lost all contact with the other companions. The strength of the projections had surrounded him, isolating him even from Iroshi.

That unaccustomed isolation did not wholly explain the most recent reaction. For half an hour they had discussed the incident, each trying to remain rational. A few minutes ago, he had gone silent, withdrawing; she did not know why.

"Ensi?"

Several times she had tried to reestablish contact without success.

"Ensi?"

Yes, Iroshi. I am here.

"What's bothering you about all of this that you're not telling me?"

Nothing. Why do you ask?

"Don't give me that male/female shit! You know damn well why I ask. There is something that's bothering you that you're not telling me. I want to know what it is."

How could she make decisions if she did not have all the available information? Even the smallest decisions affected Ensi as much as they did her. His worries were hers—even worse, when she had to guess what the problem was, she worried even more.

It is a feeling, something that is almost impossible to describe. He went silent a moment, but at least he was there and he was trying to tell her what was bothering him. *Do you believe in genetic memory?*

"No. But I don't disbelieve it, either. It's something I have no direct experience with. There have been moments of remembering something I could not know. Like it had happened before. That isn't the same thing, I guess."

Almost the same. The three of us—Garon, Savron, and I—we all have the feeling of . . . that there is a familiarity here. On this world. It is silly. But we all feel it.

"Was there anything like this on Nevas before you went into revay? Particularly the carnivores. That's the strongest element we've encountered, and they may have triggered the feeling of familiarity."

No, nothing like that. They would be very hard to forget.

"It was a long time ago."

I do not think that enough time would ever pass to erase such a memory.

"Even so, I need you with me, Ensi. I can understand that something like this can be distracting. Gods know that I don't feel like my mind is my own." She chuckled. "Funny, I felt that way once before. I don't think anything ever scared me as much as our first encounters."

A horrid thought flashed into her mind.

"Do you think these carnivores could insinuate themselves into our minds the way you did? The way the companions do? They could become a permanent part of us. That's a frightening possibility."

No, not in that way. We could not survive such an invasion.

"You mean it would kill us?"

I have no doubt. Their nature is too alien, too repulsive. Not because they are from a different world. But because they are of a much more primitive nature. The same would be true of wild carnivores on Rune-Nevas or Siebeling. Think: How often have you eaten since this all started?

She had not had a bite of food since that first night. Weakness from hunger—that might be part of the reason she was strongly affected by the contact even while awake.

"The need to protect ourselves is even greater than we realized. We have to get into the ruins, especially Mark. What does Savron say about his strength?"

He is weakening fast. It is difficult to believe that his physical wounds were so slight. Not nearly enough to cause his death.

"Is he strong enough to wait another day or so?"

Savron does not think so.

"Then we'll have to get moved this afternoon. Just the three of us for the time being. Since the others are not susceptible, they can stay here and work on the ship. If that should become too dangerous . . . well, they'll have to join us there. Maybe sleep in the ruins at night and work here during the day."

She thought a moment. Just the three of them might not be such a good idea. If the nocturnal projections did affect them within the ruins, they would need someone unaffected to help them.

"We'll take Jarys with us, too. She will have to be briefed on what to do. Not that there's much we can tell her."

They discussed the pros and cons of splitting up the group. The most compelling argument for staying together was, of course, their greater numbers being better protection. Also, there would be more hands to work on the racer. However, staying at the racer was not an option for the Glaivers. Iroshi knew instinctively that safety lay in the ruins. The others were willing to follow her.

Since their choices were somewhat limited, details were easy to plan. Particularly regarding weapons. The power was out on the ship, meaning there was no way to recharge the power packs of the guns. Erik, Iroshi, and Jarys would each take a pistol, leaving the majority of the guns for those left behind. The two Glaive members would rely more on their two swords: katanas and wakizashis. The only time these weapons became useless was when the arms became too tired to fight. Hopefully they would not need either type of weapon. So far, the carnivores had kept their distance, but their actions were unpredictable. Even seeing their thoughts was not warning enough, because no one on the ship was familiar with the terrain. Nor had Walker made an appearance. She might have gone away, leaving them to whatever doom the planet might choose.

The plans had been relayed to Erik, and he set about gathering the supplies they would need. Meanwhile, Iroshi informed Ferguson they were moving. After pointing out once again that they had no idea if the ruins were safe, he set Garrick and Donner to the task of getting Mark ready to travel. Iroshi sat down with Jarys to explain the basic problem she and the brothers were having.

Civilians within the Glaive understood that most of the members were telepathic to one degree or another. No one outside the membership knew of the symbiosis of host and companion. Some day it would get out; too many people had the knowledge for the secret to be kept forever. However, letting those who worked for the Glaive know some of the lesser secrets made them feel more a part of the organization. It also simplified the process of telling Jarys and having her understand why the decision to move had been made.

In less than an hour they were ready to leave. Erik led the way, followed by Jarys pushing the powered litter bearing his brother. Iroshi brought up the rear, pistol in hand. She turned to look back before the trees blocked the view of the ship. Garrick and Donner had already gone back inside. Ferguson stood alone at the end of the ramp. She waved, and he returned the farewell gesture.

Knowing that the walls of the ship had been repaired enough to block anything without a power weapon from getting inside did not make her feel easier about leaving them. Nor did the knowledge that with only the three of them, repairs would take so much longer. Hell, six of them were hard pressed to make any headway.

The trek proved to be slow going. She and Erik were worn out from lack of sleep, and Jarys had some difficulty maneuvering the litter across exposed roots and other obstacles in the path. The packs each carried were heavy and cumbersome. Even so, one of them would have to make the trip back after three days to secure more food and water. If the replicator, at least, was repaired by then. If Iroshi, Mark, and Erik had begun to eat by then. The emergency stores were planned for short durations—five or six days at most. No one had become so totally lost before.

Iroshi did not relish the thought of trying to live off the land. Not in competition with the carnivores who hunted at night. Nor was there any indication that those were the only carnivores on this world. Then there was the problem of actually finding anything edible.

Erik and Jarys stopped in front, bringing two hours of speculation to a close. She moved to Erik's side and looked ahead. The hill rose before them, larger than she had envisioned it from his description. Tens of thousands of people must have lived there at the height of the civilization. She considered the surrounding wall warily. In its ruined condition it would certainly prove to be no deterrent against instrusion. She studied the roads leading upward with even more trepidation.

"How far up the hill do you think we'll have to go for the best effect?" she asked Erik.

"I think you will notice a difference almost immediately. We may not have to go far in order to be protected. From the projections, that is. Protection from bad weather—if there is any—is best in the building on top. The large one with the dome." He pointed. "It's the only one with a fairly complete roof."

"For this first night I think we can stay nearer the bottom. It doesn't look like there will be any rain. We have the tarp if we need it."

Erik nodded. She turned back to Jarys.

"Are you doing all right?"

"Yes, I can make it," the medic answered. Her forehead and upper lip shone with sweat, but her breathing was regular.

"Let's go, then," Iroshi said.

She stepped to the side and again let the others lead. Before following, she checked behind and the surroundings closely. Nothing moved, not even the air. Her own upper lip felt moist, the air too humid to allow perspiration to evaporate. The reaction was from nerves as much as from exertion.

Ensi's apprehension about the ruins was catching. Even at that distance, something about the city nagged at her memories. She had explored ruins before, back on Rune-Nevas particularly. In spite of the runes, these were not at all like the temple. Were they?

Something moved in the underbrush, causing leaves to sway and rustle. She hurried to catch up.

Mark slept quietly, stretched out on the litter. Erik sat near him on a large stone that had toppled from one of the walls. Iroshi gazed across the fire, then away. As they sat waiting for something to happen, she and Erik found it increasingly difficult to meet each other's eyes. She was afraid for him to see the fear that must be reflected in her own.

Jarys had gone exploring, having promised that she would not go far and would come running at the least call from either of them. Although the hand comms did not reach back to the ship, they did work within the city's confines. The medic's intuition made her accept the seriousness of the situation even though she could not understand what it must be like. Civilians working within the Glaive were tested for any type of extrasensory perception. It seemed best to have a contingent within their ranks that would not be susceptible to outside infuences in the same way the members might be. The precaution was proving to be a wise one.

Iroshi shifted on her own stone seat from the numb cheek to the other. Still not comfortable, she stood up. It had been a long time since she had camped out. Thank goodness the fallen trees proved easy to burn and they had gathered a good supply. They had lanterns and torches for light, but there was nothing like a crackling fire over which to warm your hands in the evening chill.

Although the western sky still glowed with sunlight, she spread her sleeping bag on the ground, close to the fire. It had taken them nearly an hour to clear the ground of stones and shards of debris so that their bedding places would not be too lumpy. The bag was so inviting, her eyelids so heavy, but not yet. She would not be able to sleep until she knew if this move was going to work.

Her stomach growled, but a quick look indicated that Erik had not heard. He stood and stretched noisily, then he moved over to check his brother's pulse and watch his breathing a moment.

"There's something I didn't tell you before," he said quietly.

"What?" Iroshi asked.

"The animal that has attached itself to me. It hears the thoughts of the leader, like instructions on what to do."

"You mean, you get images from two different animals?"

"Yes. Yours . . . that is, the leader's are abbreviated, almost controlled. It tells what route it's going to take, when it's going to leap—so that the others know when and how to follow."

"Wait a minute. Does your animal transmit to any of the others?"

"Not that I can tell. But that doesn't mean anything. I mean, how could I tell?"

"I don't know. I haven't read any others' thoughts."

She paced a few minutes, then sat back down on the rock she had been using for a seat. An interesting thought had occurred to her, not that it would help them solve their problem, but it was interesting.

"Ensi, have you had any feel for how many of the animals in the pack actually transmit their thoughts?"

No, we have only been working to shield ourselves from them.

Aloud she said, "What if an animal becomes leader of the pack because she—or he—has telepathic abilities?" She stood and started pacing again. "As soon as Mark can tell us, we must know which of the animals is in contact with him. If it's one of the same ones in contact with us . . ."

Erik looked skeptical.

"Doesn't it seem strange that it appears to be a one-to-one contact? I know it might never do us any good to figure any of this out, but the more we know about them, the better chance we have of fighting the effects of their thoughts."

Both went silent. There must be ways to put such knowledge to use, but nothing specific came to mind. If they all worked on the possibilities, they were bound to come up with an idea.

"The sun's down," Erik said.

She turned to look at the horizon. From their height on the hill they could see above the surrounding trees. The whole sky was dark, stars beginning to twinkle brighter and brighter. Silence inside and out. So far.

13

❖

Birds sang morning greetings to the rising sun. The air was still cool and moist, and Iroshi snuggled deeper into the sleeping bag. Just a few more minutes of sleep, then she would get up and continue exploring the temple. It was for fun now that water had been found.

Someone coughed and she sat bolt upright. Memories of two assassins in the night made her reach for the katana.

"Good morning," a voice said. A figure hunched close to the fire, stirring coals and adding more wood.

Iroshi started breathing again. It was Jarys tending the fire, and this was not the temple ruins. That morning in the temple had occurred many years earlier.

"Good morning," she answered and undid the fastenings on the bag. "Cool morning, rather."

"Yes, it is. I thought I would get some water heating for coffee."

"Good idea."

"Did you sleep well?"

"Yes, I did."

Jarys rooted in the supply box until she found the coffee bags and boiling pot. She filled the pot from the water jug, then set it on the bed of hot coals.

Iroshi hugged her knees to her chest. She had slept well. What a blessed event. Erik and she had stayed up until past midnight, sending Jarys to bed first. Erik had been due to take second watch, but had not felt like going to sleep right away. By midnight, they knew that the move had worked. No thoughts, no projections, no hunt, not even a tickling on the edge of consciousness. Something within the ruins did block thought transference from outside its boundaries. At the same time, the companions had been unable to touch anyone back at the ship, even though they knew exactly where Ferguson and the others were. A mixed blessing, then. However, who could argue with a good night's sleep?

After Erik had gone to bed, Iroshi had reveled in the silence. She and Ensi discussed many things, even some unrelated to their present predicament, for the pure pleasure of each other's thoughts. Off and on he went quiet as he tried contact off-world but with no success. He could still contact Garon and Savron, but they were also within the city's precincts. That made them all prisoners of a sort.

By the time she woke Erik, she was tired enough to go right to sleep. No dreams of any kind had disturbed the night.

The smell of the coffee brought her to her feet. Jarys handed her a cup, and she tasted it tentatively. Hot. The first she had tasted in four mornings. And she was hungry. She told Jarys so, but the medic had anticipated her and was already putting together a meal.

"We'll wake Erik when it's ready," Iroshi said.

She walked over to Mark and checked him over. His

pulse was stronger, although his color was still quite
pale. His mouth was relaxed rather than pulled into a
thin line as it had been. Progress at last.

When they woke Erik, he was also hungry. He and
Iroshi wolfed down the reconstituted food, and she
thought of asking Jarys to fix another helping. She considered their limited supplies and decided against it.
Amazing how regaining an appetite could be such an encouraging sign; she found herself looking forward to the
day's activities.

The night before, they had planned for her and Jarys
to begin exploring the ruins while Erik stayed with his
brother. The two women strapped on hand comms and
started off. Jarys would start on this street, checking
buildings on both sides until she had made the full circuit. Then she would go to the next street up the hill and
repeat the process.

Meanwhile, Iroshi would climb to the top to check out
the large, domed building that Erik had described as so
complete. Its survival might mean that the damping
mechanism, if it existed, was there. If she was lucky,
there would be no subterranean chambers to check out.
Or fall into.

As she climbed, she could not help remembering the
incident in the temple complex that had confirmed for
all time that she suffered from claustrophobia. It had
been a sunny day, and she had been searching for a
source of water. The floor giving way under her. The
drop twenty feet into darkness and a pool of cold water.
Nothing else, before or since, had ever frightened her as
much as that fall into utter darkness. Finding her way

out had thoroughly tested her courage and her ability to survive. Nor had she ever felt more alone. She had not known that she was not alone; nor that she would never be alone again.

Every so often, in times of great stress, the dreams would come back. The feeling of falling, the fear of being trapped.

She tripped over a crack between stones in the roadway. Better stop that train of thought and quickly, or she might fall even without the floor giving way from underneath. These ruins were enough of a task without revisiting old ones.

The elevation of the climb was more gradual than it looked at first. She kept her eye on the building that was her goal, when not looking down at the road. The closer she got, the greater the tension gripping her body. Not just her tension; Ensi's too. Did the companions expect to find something from their own pasts here? Or fear to find it? How could they know for sure *if* they found it?

At last she stood in the doorway, the darkness beyond uninviting. Pulling the torch from her belt, she thumbed the switch. Its narrow beam did not help build enthusiasm. Once inside, the darkness was not quite as absolute as it had seemed. Although the morning sun was still low, some light found its way inside through the open side of the dome. The beam of the upraised torch lit the solid half of the dome, revealing something that Erik had missed or had not recognized: hinges and other mechanical bits still clung to the plaster. The missing part of the dome had been designed to open.

"Astronomical observations," she said silently.

Yes, Ensi said. *An observatory.*

"An odd place to set up a telescope, isn't it?"

Without knowing the history, who can tell? Perhaps it was the first one in the city and, as they built newer and better equipment, they left it here for children to experience looking at the heavens.

"You think this might have been something like a museum, then?"

I have no idea as yet.

Of course not. No one could, with so little to go on. Iroshi massaged a slight crick in her neck from looking up and moved to the right. Several doors were set in the wall, all closed or nearly so. A different kind of door appeared in the walls on both sides of the main entrance. Unlike the others that were hinged, swinging doors, these had slid into the wall. A quick search did not reveal any sort of handhold with which to open them. However, she suspected they were probably elevator doors, something that would be impossible to use without power, and positively unsafe in any case, as old as they were.

Most of the runes had been carved in the wall nearest the wide corridor leading toward the rear of the building and she turned toward them. With the help of the torch, even she could read an occasional word, so similar were they to the inscriptions on Rune-Nevas.

This means a relationship of some kind with my people.

"Since your people never achieved spaceflight, it would seem that these people came to Nevas."

Possibly. Whether to visit or colonize, we will never know.

"There might be some kind of record here that would tell us something."

What? Do you believe they would have left behind an account of their civilization just in case someone should stop by in the distant future?

"Why not? Especially if that civilization was dying. Maybe they just all packed up and left. Some great odyssey to the stars."

And left some great damping machine running to keep telepathic peoples from being able to communicate? And a city that is within that damping field so the animals left behind could live free from fear of the carnivores?

"Clearly, we haven't enough information to know who these people were and what their relationship may have been to your people or to this world, for that matter. I don't think we'll find all the answers here, either."

She moved along the wall, careful to avoid the few large stones littering the floor, scanning each inscription, studying each star chart. Most of the charts were unfamiliar since she had not studied the stars from this vantage point in the galaxy. Ensi quieted, studying along with her.

"We'll have to come back and make copies of each of these, and photograph them."

Ensi agreed. However, their first priority at the moment was to see if the damping mechanism was within the confines of the building. Since it was the largest and tallest construction in the city, and assuming the machine would be of some size, it seemed a logical place to start.

"Let's see if we can find some stairs," she said softly.

The corridor looked long and dark. No light crept in from outside. One hand holding the torch and the other resting on the butt of her pistol, she started down.

The sound of her footsteps was muffled by the layer of dust, deeper here than in the rotunda. The corridor must act like a wind tunnel when the wind was up outside, drawing wind and the dust it carried along its length. That would mean an exit of some kind at the other end, now invisible in black shadows. That exit should be a staircase; the next hope was that the staircase was intact, not impossible since much of this building had thus far survived whatever ravages there were on this world.

Several doors on either side appeared within the gloom. If the machinery was not located on the upper floors, every floor would have to be searched. Not a pleasant prospect.

A breeze sighed behind her, caressed her back, moved gently around as if she were a stone in a stream. Ripples sparkled in the beam from the torch, created by dust particles to be added to the layer underfoot. Larger pieces of debris—dry leaves and twigs—rattled against the dirt layer and walls as their positions were changed once more.

The corridor was longer than she had guessed, and she fought back the urge to hurry. A basement could not be darker. The only encouragement was the walls on either side, close enough that the light touched them, giving a sense of width at least, if not one of length.

I do not believe there is one living thing besides you in this whole building, Ensi said softly. *I have touched nothing at all.*

Creatures were not what she feared most; but his voice in her head helped lessen the rising claustrophobia that always threatened her in places like this.

"Will the damping field keep other living creatures out of here? I mean, we're assuming that the carnivores can't get within the city, aren't we? But we got in. What is the difference?"

The primitive nature of their minds would be my guess. But you are right. We do not know if the field actually keeps them outside the walls. Further, we do not know that the field keeps out their thought projections. All we do know is that we experienced none last night.

"Thanks a lot, Ensi. I was just starting to feel better."

She stopped abruptly. Directly in front of her was the opening in the corridor that she had been looking for. Within an alcove on the other side was what looked like stairs. The darkness was so deep that it absorbed the light until she was almost on top of the quarry.

The feeling of surprise gone, she stepped up onto a landing. To the right, stairs disappeared downward. Damn, there *was* a basement. To the left, stairs led upward. She leaned over the balustrade, careful not to put any weight against it, and shone the light up. Nothing except stairs and balustrade disappearing into more darkness.

"We did agree to start on the top floor, right?"

Correct. It is the most logical . . .

"I remember."

It felt like she had already spent hours in the building, although it could not have been more than half an hour. An hour at most. Facing five opponents with swords was far more desirable than searching through one deserted building. But search she must.

"Have you told Garon and Erik?"

Yes. I will be in constant touch with Garon as long as we are separated.

That answered another question: contact between the two companions had not been cut off by a combination of distance and damping field. Time to start climbing.

She adjusted the katana slung across her back and took the first step. When she shone the light upward, the staircase rose in a wide spiral and seemed to be complete. Like the walls, stone was used here, although cut differently—smooth but unpolished. Of course, the polish would have been worn away by years of traffic and centuries of scouring by wind and dust. Even without the polish, the dust made the steps slightly slippery, and she not only tested with her weight, but she also placed her foot firmly with each step.

There is something ahead.

She had almost reached the second floor. She stopped and listened carefully for any sound other than her own breathing.

I cannot locate it exactly. Nor can I tell what it is. It is something alive but . . . but almost mindless.

"Is it near or far?"

I do not know. It is moving.

"Is it dangerous?"

*I do not know. I can tell nothing about it except . . .
The carnivores' thought processes are ruled by instinct.
Their minds are very basic, but they do have primitive
thought processes. This new thing does not think.*

They would have to assume that it was dangerous.
Next question: sword or pistol? If she drew either one,
she would not be able to grip the banister and hold the
torch as well. At least not securely. A scraping sound
came from above. Second floor? Higher?

Walker tried the comm one more time. No use. Communication between the planet's surface and the ship orbiting overhead was completely lost. No surprise, since
they had not been able to use any of the sensors in either
the ship or the shuttle to locate the Glaive racer. She
would send word back with the shuttle for the ship to
keep the jammer off but to continue monitoring for any
outbound signals.

People and supplies had been unloaded, boxes stacked
a few feet away, the mercenaries standing alertly with
their weapons ready.

"All right, Greg," Walker said to the shuttle pilot.
"We'll see you back here in two hours with the next
load."

She climbed out and went to stand near the group
while she watched the shuttle lifted off. As soon as it was clear, she
turned to Andretti.

"Send someone into the woods with a hand comm and
see how far he goes before we lose contact," she ordered.

Andretti nodded and turned to relay the order. That was the way orders should be obeyed: promptly and without question. She had learned that from Duncan.

Another mercenary was set to monitoring all comm frequencies for any transmissions from the racer. They knew from its downward trajectory that the Glaive ship had to be within a thirty-mile radius of where they had unloaded. Triangulation on a radio wave would be a lot easier than searching on foot.

If they were lucky—very lucky—they might even have a direction by the time the next group was landed. That might be expecting too much, but it would simplify things so wonderfully. Of course, if the Glaivers had stayed together at the ship, there would not even be a transmission; however, chances were that someone would be sent away once in a while to check on one thing or another. What such a "thing" might be she could only imagine: water, food, other supplies that might be found locally?

Then again, no transmission could mean the Glaivers were all dead. A more pleasant possibility, but somehow less likely.

Crouching slightly apart from the others, Graham checked over the rifles, her hands sure and her knowledge complete and invaluable. She had once roamed among worlds as one of those ronin after spending ten years with some army employed by a corporation on a distant world; the name of either long forgotten. After the corporation came under new management, the army was disbanded, its leaders executed. The effect on Graham must have been almost as devastating as Duncan's death had been. However, Graham had managed to convince herself that it was just one of the downsides of her profession. She had said as much on the few occasions they had talked.

After taking over the management of Duncan's business when he died, Walker had put Graham in charge of the paramilitary force he had started. Increasing its size and effectiveness had become an obsession. In addition, she had hired instructors in all forms of martial arts, had taken most courses of study herself, and took pride in being a good student. That was something Duncan had never done. He had left the fighting to those he hired for the purpose, saving his energies for other pursuits.

It did not matter that Duncan had beaten her on a fairly regular basis. She had deserved it nearly every time. But Walker was damned if another man would do the same for any reason.

She watched as camp was set up. No supervision needed; they knew their jobs and did them automatically.

Walker sat down on a fallen tree and leaned back against another. She had a lot to be proud of and more on its way. Self-satisfaction was not a bad thing.

14

✦

Another scraping sound echoed off the walls and up and down the shaft. Iroshi placed her right foot on the next step very carefully. Don't slip. Don't make a sound.

She had moved from the outside of the staircase to the inside, against the wall. The view up the stairs was a little longer from that side, but the way the staircase spiraled, that did not mean a great deal. Light from the torch only went so far, leaving much—too much—in darkness. Especially now that a thing lay somewhere in that darkness.

Friend or foe? Tiger or pussycat? Ensi could not tell; the thing's mind was too basic. She could not tell because she could not see, hear, or smell it. Well, its movements made occasional sound. Odd that she was so sure that the sounds were of movement rather than the creature's stomach rumbling or some other inane sound.

The sword in her left hand glinted as she moved the torch from side to side. Another reason she had moved to the inside of the staircase: she could lean her shoulder against the wall to help maintain balance, hold the torch in her left hand, and the sword in her right hand. Although the gun had greater range, the sword was at least as practical since her eyesight, under current conditions, did not have much range. Besides, the weight of the sword was more satisfying, more encouraging.

More primitive too, in keeping with the character of the creature up there. Maybe.

She reached the second-floor landing. The last few steps had taken an eternity. Exaggeration. Better watch it—might be a sign of getting old.

More sounds from above. Either the thing had been on the third floor all along or it had climbed ahead of her.

The torchlight revealed no tracks in the dust. So. It was big enough for its movements to be heard almost two floors below. Of course, the utter silence of the building helped.

"You've told Garon what's going on?"

Yes. I am keeping everyone informed as we move along. We are moving, are we not?

"Fast enough to satisfy me."

Over the years, Ensi had gotten in the habit of teasing her at moments like this to help ease the tension. Sometimes it worked, sometimes it did not. At the moment, it was not working. All of her life she had battled with claustrophobia, darkness being her nemesis, where one cannot find the way out of danger. This fear never went away, although she handled it. Not much else to do, really.

Halfway up the last flight of stairs. The noises came more often, receding and approaching. Like some great mass walking the floor in anticipation. Or gliding on the floor. Or crawling. Eight steps left.

It might know she was coming. It might be able to see, hear, or smell her. Five steps left.

At last she stood on the landing. Nothing directly in front. She leaned against the alcove wall, swung the torch to catch the other side on the right of the entry. Nothing there, not even a wall near enough to catch the light. She skipped to the right wall of the alcove, shone the torch in the opposite direction with the same result.

The scraping sound came again, this time from the left. Not real close. She moved outside the alcove to the opposite side of the wall, shone the torch around again. Nothing caught the light, either living, dead, or indifferent. That aroused curiosity about this floor: was it divided into a number of rooms like the other two floors, or was it just one big room? Maybe a smaller number of rooms, all large, Meeting rooms. Equipment rooms.

Better investigate the creature first. Either it needed to be eliminated completely, if it was dangerous, or she needed to know that it was not dangerous.

All right. Move left. Keep close to the wall.

In the far distance, a hole in the corner of the building let in a small amount of light. Not entirely dark. Switching off the torch for a moment, she stood quite still, letting her eyes adjust until she could almost see. That was the west side of the building. In the afternoons, then, the amount of light should increase. That brought the temptation to come back later in the day to find out what the creature was. However, it might be difficult to make herself come up those stairs again, knowing that something was here.

Features within the space began to stand out black

against grey. Then she made out a large mass almost backlit by the illumination from the hole in wall and ceiling. The edges wavered in and out of perception, seeming to flutter. An illusion. No. The right edge actually moved, an undulating motion. No, again. Only a part of that edge. The uppermost part did not move. Assume the movement was the creature?

It might be. Although the thing is closer than it was, I simply cannot tell.

"Is there no concentration of its mind?"

No concentration whatever. We could be inside it for all I can tell.

She switched the torch back on. Still too far away for it to help much. Okay, let's get closer.

First, check the floor ahead. No obstacles, just more dust and dirt. Moving forward, she fought back the urge to cough. A few steps and she stopped. Was that a vibration in the floor? With her boot she scuffed dust aside until the entire sole touched the floor itself. Yes, the floor was vibrating slightly. A machine vibration. Power.

"Could the vibration come from the creature?" she asked, wanting to be sure.

No, I do not think so. You are right that it is a machine vibration. However, I am sensing something else. Like a heartbeat, perhaps, or breathing. Straight ahead.

She moved forward again. Sweat was beginning to make her hands slick. No problem with the katana with its leather-wrapped handle, but the torch was high-impact plastic. She stopped a moment, tucked the torch under her other arm, and rubbed the palm of her left hand on her tunic. Better. Time to get this over with.

Rising dust made her throat scratchy, and it was getting harder not to cough. There seemed to be no way to step without disturbing the layers on the floor. There also seemed to be no way to get closer to the mass rising from the floor ahead without risking detection. The third floor, at least on this side of the stairs, must be one big room. That put the machine or creature or both at least fifty feet away.

She swallowed, but a cough exploded into the silence. Followed by another. Something within the mass ahead moved. Two pinpoints of red shone within it. Could be eyes reflecting light from the torch. Eyes about eight feet off the floor. Nice. That meant it was big. Why couldn't it be lights on the side of the machine? The glowing spots moved. Okay, not from the machine.

Conquering the coughing spell, she moved closer, still keeping one shoulder touching the wall for balance. A hiss broke the new silence, threatening. The hair rose on the back of her neck.

"I'll be right there," Jarys's voice said over the comm unit.

Erik fidgeted. He could not leave Mark alone, and Jarys was nearly on the other side of the hill. It would take her ten, fifteen minutes to get back in spite of the straight-line streets.

Meanwhile, Iroshi was stalking—or being stalked by—some creature whose nature was totally unknown.

She had not ordered him to come, but Ensi had strongly suggested that she might need his help.

Knowing her reputation, she would probably use the sword rather than the gun. More than once members of the Glaive had speculated that their leader had a death wish; at least this weapon preference seemed to indicate that. Sure, the sword could be the ideal weapon under certain circumstances, but this did not sound like one of those times.

He reached down for the jury-rigged barbells—two water drums tied to each end of a tent pole—and started doing military presses. Working out was calming, one of the few activities that made waiting possible. He switched to arm curls and had completed five sets of those when he heard someone coming down the road. After setting the barbells down, he drew the pistol from the holster at his side and stepped into the street.

The sun was nearly at its zenith, its warmth adding to the heat of his body. The sunshine made the sweat on his large arms glisten.

The sounds came from his right. He stepped into the shadows of a corner of the building and waited for the runner to appear. Only a moment went by, and Jarys burst into sight. She did not see Erik at first and shrieked when he stepped into view. Sliding to a stop, she nearly ran right into him. He holstered the gun.

"Mark's sleeping," he told her as they went inside. Erik grabbed his sword and belt and a bag holding three torches. "We'll be in touch." He started toward the door, then turned back. "Don't leave him."

Jarys nodded breathlessly, and Erik went out the door

and started up the hill at a trot. Mark had improved since their arrival yesterday, and nothing must interfere with his recovery. However, other matters must be seen to.

Even his powerful legs tired from the pace he set, and he slowed to a fast walk. In another few minutes, he stood at the entrance of the building. It yawned black against the grey stone of the walls.

Hurry, Ensi said. *It is about to begin.*

The room had brightened slightly as the sun neared its zenith. Once it started down toward the western horizon, the brightness should increase greatly. The closer she got to the machine and its companion, the greater was the vibration in the floor. Now she could even hear a slight hum in the air, which could almost be mistaken for a cat's purr.

The creature's form intermingled with the machine's so that it was difficult to discern where one began and the other ended. Both sat nearly in the center of the room, and by staying close to the wall, she approached from the front and was now working around one side toward the rear. The pair of eyes—if that was what they were—followed, winking off and on as they blinked or the light source moved. Hard to tell which, or maybe both.

Just a moment earlier Ensi had told her he had sent for Erik. He was supposed to be bringing as many torches as he could carry. Of course, they had only brought eight from the racer. After all, there were four of them, each having two hands. How many more could they have needed?

The thing hissed again, reminiscent of a snake even though she had seen only one in her whole life and that was many years ago. That one had been a harmless species kept in Mushimo's gardens to take care of rodents that occasionally invaded it. Harmless or not, the thing had threatened her when she stumbled across it. Only Mushimo's intervention had kept her from killing it with her sword. He had scolded her for being so eager to kill, and as punishment made her read every book in his library with references to snakes. She still did not like them any more than she liked this thing confronting her now.

Even so, she hesitated. What right had she to kill this snake thing? She was the invader, the intruder. However, she must get to the machine in order to see if it was the source of the damping effect and, if so, figure out how to control it. When it came to survival, she could be ruthless.

It will not listen to reason, Ensi said.

"I don't see any way around the problem except to kill it. Even though it might be perfectly harmless."

At that size, it is dangerous whether it wants to be or not. Our survival must come first.

His words surprised her. Ordinarily he was not ruthless, but he did have reason to want to study this building, and the culture it represented, without interference.

While this exchange had gone on, she had edged closer, testing the reaction of the snake. The head raised, the red of the eyes steady in her direction. She held perfectly still. Did it strike like a snake? Was its body long enough to reach her?

With the light closer and its head raised, exposing more of its body, its skin looked a dull red. Four feet from the tip of its nose, little feelers or legs sprouted from each side. Possibly its means of locomotion.

The rest of its body was entwined among the parts of the machine—or what looked like parts of the machine. Even this close, it was difficult to separate the two in the darkness.

"Does it like the heat from the machine, or is it the vibrations?"

I wish I knew. That would give us a point to work from.

"Any way you can figure out how it knows where I am? Does it see me or smell my breath?"

There is nothing coming from this creature. It is as if it does not have a brain at all.

"Like an earthworm," Iroshi murmured. Only the head was more distinctive.

She took a small step to the right. The head turned an instant later, keeping her directly in front of it. Whether it sensed sound or movement, or both, it was quite conscious of her presence and position. She dashed closer, struck it with the flat of her sword. The metal smacked as it hit dry skin. She leapt back. The head stretched toward her, snapped back to its previous position like it was on an elastic band. It was faster than she thought it would be. There went the half-formed plan of luring it from the machine, then racing around it to flip a switch or whatever one could find to turn the mechanism off.

Dammit! She did not want to kill the beast if she did

not have to. However, it was looking more and more like she would have to.

She dashed in again, hit it, leapt back. This time the mouth opened when it lunged toward her, revealing a full row of very sharp teeth, both upper and lower. It hissed, enveloping her in fetid breath that nearly gagged her. She stumbled farther back, desperate for a clear breath.

What could it possibly feed on inside the building? Especially a creature of that size.

Although it elongated when it lunged, at rest the thing appeared to be about five feet in diameter. The jaws were three feet wide, maybe a little more. Difficult to tell with the curvature.

She crept closer, then lunged again. The huge mouth opened and the blade struck teeth with a clang. The creature hissed and lunged in turn. Iroshi scrambled backward, slipping in the dust. The creature's refusal to loose its hold on the machine was all that kept it from grabbing her in those jaws. Next time it might let go. Better be more careful.

Warily, she struck twice more before it loosened its hold on the machine. The third time its full length let go, landing on the floor with a dull plop. A cloud of dust filled the air, and she raced backward. It was a moment before she could see it again. Its head swayed back and forth, clearly looking for her. She ran around behind and smacked it near the tail, where its diameter was much less. The snake turned and struck, but in the dust it had less traction, the little legs practically spinning. The whole creature was surprisingly short, about fifteen feet or so.

She teased it farther from the center of the room. It hissed more frequently in obvious frustration. Between the dust filling the air from their moving around and the snake's breath, she found it harder and harder to breathe. Better get to the business of examining the machinery.

She bolted for it, running and then sliding the last ten feet, banging hard into the mechanical bulk. Hand and fingertips found many buttons and switches protruding from the otherwise flat surface, but none that felt like power switches. Nothing on the end, either. She started to work around to the other side, but the snake was moving in fast.

"Iroshi," someone shouted from the stairway.

"Erik, here." She shone the torch in his direction.

"Got it," he shouted.

"Careful, the floor's slick."

She circled, using the machine like a shield. The snake was getting angrier by the minute, and it crawled up one side.

Damn, it was back on the machine. All that work for nothing.

Erik's torch beam closed in.

"See if you can lure it away, Erik. It's pretty fast. Be careful. It surprises you once in a while. Hit it with the flat of your sword to get its attention."

He ran up and smacked it from behind. The snake turned its head quickly, but Erik had moved even faster.

"It's got teeth," he said.

"Yes."

No sign of switches or anything resembling a control on the second side, either. Only the other end left to check. What if the controls were behind a panel? Could she spot it? Yes, there. A seam outlining a square in the dark metallic case. Nothing to pull it open with. Maybe it pushed. She tried all four sides. Nothing. The corners, then.

The panel popped down when she pushed the right upper corner. The torch shone on two slide controls inside with writing over each.

"Ensi, can you read the labels?"

It . . . Yes, I think I can. It is older than our writing on Nevas.

Well, that answered two questions. He had been quiet about the inscriptions on the walls, she had assumed because he was gathering as much information as possible before making a judgment. Now she knew that he could not only read them, but that they were possibly the ancestor of the runes on Rune-Nevas.

"What do they say?"

The top one—you understand that the meaning could actually be entirely different from what I read—identifies that switch as the power switch. The lower one regulates the strength of the output. There is nothing, however, that says this is the damping field control.

"Top is power switch and bottom is volume or whatever you want to call it?" She touched each with a fingertip. To her right, Erik swore. A quick glance to be sure he was all right. "Let's turn it off, shall we?"

The slide sat nearly all the way to the right. Left to turn it off, maybe?

"Nothing says 'on' and 'off'?"

No.

"Here goes."

She pushed the switch all the way to the left. At first nothing seemed to have happened. Then she felt it. Or did not feel. The vibration in the floor was gone. More clearly, her fingertips detected the loss of energy within the cabinet.

"Does this seem too easy?"

Yes. Be grateful until we have reason to fear otherwise. Even if this works, we cannot leave it off. That would allow the carnivores' hunting forays to reach you again.

"I know. Right now, I just want to know if we can control the field."

She stepped around the machine, trying to locate Erik and his adversary. The man stood with his back to her in the far left corner. The creature was cornered, hissing and gnashing its teeth.

"Don't kill it," she yelled.

"What?"

"I don't want to kill it if we don't have to. Let's get out of here."

"I don't understand," Erik said, but he backed away as he spoke.

While the snake remained in the corner, its head swaying side to side, she headed for the stairway. Erik stopped beside Iroshi and the two of them stood looking at the creature a moment.

"I think I've gotten the machine turned off," she said softly. "If that thing is here only because of the machine, it might leave now. There's no warmth or vibration for it to stay attached to."

She put her hand on Erik's arm.

"Let's go downstairs and wait."

She sneezed twice. That seemed to wake the snake from whatever trance it had been in; it surged forward, then slowed. By the light of both torches they could see its insufficient legs seeking a purchase in the dust-covered floor. They turned and raced for the staircase. She slid through the alcove opening, catching herself on the banister. In a few more minutes, and after several slips, they had descended to the first floor.

They sat on the bottom step catching their breath. She explained that they would have to turn the machine back on toward evening. They were taking a terrible chance that it would even come back on.

"Try to contact the racer on your hand comm," she said.

He called the ship three times before an answer came back.

"It took a minute to get over the shock," Ferguson's voice said.

"Do you still have the mayday signal on automatic broadcast?" Iroshi asked.

"Yes, we never turned it off, just in case."

"Good. Hopefully it's getting out now."

She explained to him about turning the machine back on later in the day. To be on the safe side, she wanted to allow at least an hour for it to warm up, or whatever it might need to do.

"What about the creature up there?" Erik asked when

they had signed off. Both had been glancing over their shoulders in apprehension. "How is it going to get out of the building, if it does decide to leave?"

They turned to look as a noise echoed down the shaft.

"Down the stairs?" Iroshi suggested.

15

❖

Setting up the camp was complete, down to the two-man tents. The men would have slept on the ground if she had decided they should, but she hated showy, macho exhibitions. And she sure as hell was not going to sleep on the bloody ground herself.

Andretti came running from the other side of the camp. He stopped just in front of her.

"We've made contact with the cruiser," he reported.

"How?"

"The damping effect cleared up. Reason unknown."

"Tell the captain to reestablish the jamming transmissions. If we can get through, so can the Glaivers."

He nodded and ran back to the main comm setup. In a moment he returned.

"They were making some adjustments to the equipment. The jammer will be back on soon."

"Good. Let me know if they pick up any transmissions from down here."

Andretti nodded and returned to monitoring the comm. If the racer was broadcasting on a continuous basis, they may have gotten through. If not, they probably missed their chance. Either way, she should be able to get her business done and be gone before anyone could come to the rescue.

Walker slipped into her tent to lie down for a short while. Everything was not coming together as quickly as she had hoped, but it would do. She lay down on the cot and began ticking off her advantages in her head.

Her force was larger than the Glaivers'—first advantage. She knew they were on this planet, while they had no hint that she and her people were here—second advantage. The cruiser could jam any transmissions from the racer indefinitely—third advantage. The cruiser was undamaged—fourth advantage.

Clearly, the deck was stacked in her favor. The trick was not to lose the advantages she had while grabbing others.

She turned onto her side so she could see Duncan's picture sitting on top of the case beside her. He seemed to be frowning, disapproving. Had she forgotten something?

A commotion outside indicated that one of the scouting parties had returned. She got up, looked at the picture once more, and shook her head. She could not have forgotten anything. Still, he frowned.

The scout leader was making his report to Graham when Walker stepped into the sunlight.

". . . nothing so far," he said.

Graham nodded and instructed the three to get something to eat. She started organizing the next group when she spotted her boss. Walker nodded and started back inside. She changed her mind and swung around the tent.

Maybe a long walk would restore the good feeling she had lost so suddenly.

A knock came on the door; then it swung open before Mitchell could invite the visitor inside. The racer's captain stepped in leaving the door open behind him.

"We think we just picked up part of a message from Iroshi's racer," he said excitedly.

Mitchell jumped to his feet. At last, something more to use in their search besides the information Yail had provided.

"It didn't last long, but it gave us a general direction."

"What do you mean, 'It didn't last long'?" Mitchell asked.

"It was only part of a message. The automatic distress signal that is repeated at six-second intervals."

"You're sure that it was Iroshi's racer, then?"

"We caught the end of the signal," the captain explained. "The identification code was intact. It was hers, all right."

"Get ready to feed the information to the Galician ship. I'll contact them first and let Jiron Yail know what's happened."

The captain saluted and left the cabin, closing the door behind him. Mitchell's hand shook as he manipulated the comm controls on his desk.

"We've heard from Iroshi's racer," he told Yail as soon as he answered.

The young man's smile showed he was as excited by the news as Mitchell felt. After the meager details were passed and discussed, they agreed that it was not much, but it was the first positive occurrence since the search had begun. Yail acknowledged receipt of the sketchy co-ordinates, and the two ships turned in the general direction of the signal. Until something stronger came their way, it was the best they could do. They could not even enter hyperspace to speed things up.

Mitchell pleaded work to be done and signed off. If they talked much longer, the pleasant hope that had gripped him would be totally lost in the recounting of negatives. Admittedly the signal was not much to go on, but it was more than they had found so far on their own.

For the first time, he hoped—hoped they would find Iroshi alive and unharmed; that everyone else on the racer was alive. What he did not hope for was a con-frontation with Iroshi concerning Yail. Such a con-frontation might make her feel she had to choose between them and he was not sure he would come out the winner.

There was too much to lose: his lover, his job, every-thing that gave him a reason to live. Although, by all yardsticks, he was still in his prime, he felt too old to start all over.

Stop that, he told himself. There certainly was no use in anticipating a problem that might never unfold.

The comm buzzed. Mitchell switched it on, and the captain appeared on the screen.

"Two more racers will be joining us within the next three days," he reported. "They are coming from differ-ent directions, which helps. If . . . *When* the signal comes again, we can triangulate its source and have a better chance of finding the lost ship."

"Thank you, Captain."

The face on the screen smiled its tight little smile, and the screen went blank. The other ships would have truthsayers or warriors on board, which would help further in locating the source of the signal. He thumbed the comm on again and punched the codes for Sheff's cabin. The Glaive member answered almost immediately.

"We just had a signal over the comm from Iroshi's racer," Mitchell informed him. "Did you get anything at the same time?"

He never tried to separate the host and the companion when he spoke with a member of the Glaive. Treating each bonded pair as a single entity simplified things for him and never gave hints to outsiders of the duality of a Glaive member. To everyone's knowledge, Mitchell was the only nonmember who knew of the bonding.

"Yes, a partial transmission. I think from Savron. Since everyone else is maintaining silence, it almost had to be from someone on the missing racer."

"Contact Gregory on Rune-Nevas and see if they picked up anything there."

Sheff nodded, and the screen went blank. The comm signaled, and Sheff's image reappeared.

"They received the same thing I did, except not quite as strong, of course. It was enough to begin a triangulation so that we can start in the right direction."

Mitchell nodded.

"Oh," Sheff added with a chuckle, "Gregory wanted to know how the special triangulator is working."

Mitchell grinned in spite of himself. He had brought a useless piece of equipment on board, claiming it to be a new, sophisticated triangulator that should help in the search. In reality, it was just a ruse to explain any information he might get from Gregory or other Glaivers.

"Oh, it picked up the same thing as the ship's equipment," he said, looking at the case sitting in one corner.

It was hooked up to the ship's power, and it even hummed every once in a while. The ruse was more for the Galician ship and crew than for racer crews, who had grown accustomed to impossible pronouncements at various times.

"I'd like to chuck it out into space. The damn thing takes up a lot of room in here."

"Make sure your next racer has a larger cabin for you to use."

"Sure. And I'll make sure it's right next to yours, so you won't have so much room."

They closed communication, both of them laughing at the joke that had taken three men to get on board. It was a shame that tricks had to be used, but it was better than letting too much information about the Glaive become general knowledge. Too bad they had not practiced better security in other areas.

The smile faded, but the laughter had lightened his spirits a little. There had been so little pleasure lately.

Shaking his head, he turned back to the work spread over the desktop. He had brought a lot along, hoping that it would help keep him and his mind occupied, prevent his thoughts from conjuring worst-case scenarios out of the air. So far, the effort had not helped much.

He shoved his chair back and stood up. He should have let Iroshi or one of the other warriors teach him one of the martial arts. At least he would have physical activity to occupy his mind. He flopped onto the bunk face down.

He would miss her if anything had happened . . . Don't think that way. Nothing had happened or was going to happen to her. Yeah, right. He had lived with the possibilities for years. The last ten or so, Iroshi had taken to the field less and less. He had become the administrator almost immediately in their professional relationship. He had asked her only once not to leave Rune-Nevas on assignment, and she had patiently pointed out to him that she could hardly send people out without occasionally going herself. Even if it was only to keep up with recent developments. Not that she went off-planet as a warrior or truthsayer. She was the head of the Glaive, after all, and that would not have been proper.

Not like the first six or seven years, when there were few members and she had been so intent on establishing the Glaive's reputation. Then she had been gone more often than not. Funny, he did not remember worrying so much in those days. They were younger, and Rune-Nevas itself was not entirely safe.

Suddenly he felt that Iroshi was in grave danger. Not immediate danger, but threatened by something, an ax that had not yet fallen. He sat up, his heart beating wildly, his breathing rapid. He wasn't telepathic, nor had he ever exhibited any extrasensory talents at all, but this feeling was all too real and would not go away.

16

❖❖
❖

"We're still being jammed?" Iroshi asked. "I had hoped that once we had the machine turned off, we would be able to signal off-planet."

"It isn't the damping field," Ferguson replied. "This is the jamming from off-planet. Probably Walker's ship still in orbit."

They had been trying to reach each other over the comm for some time. After the initial contact earlier in the day, everything had gone blank again, although with plenty of static.

"We may have gotten part of the distress signal out before the new block went up," Ferguson continued after a long pause. "Nothing came in."

Then there was no way to be sure that any signal actually went out. Or that anyone was even listening.

"Keep the signal broadcasting," Iroshi said. "The fact that we're able to get each other every so often means that the ship up there may be having problems with their jammer. I hope so."

"When are you planning to turn the damper back on?"

"About an hour before dark. We'll leave camp about an hour before that. We may need that extra hour to get us up there."

"We'll keep the channel open to you so we can try to determine how often . . ."

Static replaced his voice.

"Ferguson," she called. "Captain Ferguson."

No use. The jamming was back in place. At least the racer was no farther away than a short walk and, if an emergency came up, they could reach each other fairly quickly. Still, it was inconvenient.

No one doubted the signal came from Walker's ship. The prospect of her watching and waiting was not reassuring. That she might actively try to see that no one from the racer survived was not outside the realm of possibility. So, carnivores, humans, and one humongous snake, all trying for one reason or another to make sure she and her compatriots died here. Or for no real reason at all.

To the west, the sun lowered toward the horizon. She and Erik had been resting on the porch of the building for half an hour. The day had been quite an adventure. She smiled. That was a mild way of putting it.

The snake had not lingered long after the machine was turned off. A fair-weather lover. Erik and she had hidden behind one of the side doors, keeping it open far enough to see most of the rotunda and much of the corridor. The creature had appeared not long after, giving them their first opportunity to see its whole shape. Calling it a snake was about as close as one could get to a resemblance.

Except it was not long and thin; true, not all terran snakes were either. It did not have a tongue that tasted the air periodically. Its eyes were not lidless; it even seemed to have eyelashes. The short, fine appendages along each of its sides rotated, pushing or pulling it forward; they moved so fast it was impossible to tell which. It held its head upright when it moved, where most snakes stayed flatter to the ground.

Mostly, it was enormous. Her estimate of its size had not been far off: at least five feet in diameter and between fifteen and twenty feet long. Clouds of dust had risen into the air as it passed through the rotunda, and Erik could not hold back a sneeze. The two of them squeezed back when it stopped and looked around for the source of the sound. In a moment, they could hear it moving again. A quick peek around the door showed that it had resumed its trek toward the door.

As soon as it disappeared into the open, they left the doorway and followed. When they reached the porch, the creature was already out of sight. Its trail in the dust led south, away from their camp below, and they followed to make sure it actually went away. A loud hiss came to them once as it made its way down the street. It almost sounded like an agonized sigh, but that was probably lending feelings to the snake that it could not feel. Still, it had lost something to which it was clearly attached.

Well, if everything went well, they would be gone soon and it could come back. She planned to leave the machine on when they finally left; everything as it was when they first set foot on this world, or as nearly as possible.

Once the damper was turned off, they had talked to Ferguson until something else cut them off. It was only a few minutes ago that contact had been reestablished. Between times, she and Erik had returned to the camp to check on Mark. Having the damper off did not seem to have an adverse effect on him. In fact, just the opposite, as he seemed to be asleep rather than unconscious—Jarys verified that—and he opened his eyes by mid-afternoon.

That was when Iroshi realized how time was running together. For a while she tried to figure out how long since the crash, but that exercise had been depressing. Then she had decided that it did not matter; surviving was the only important thing. With that settled, she set herself and the others to tasks. Jarys started exploring lower levels while Iroshi went on up the hillside. At five they would all meet back at camp to check in; then Jarys would stay with Mark, while Erik and Iroshi returned to the building.

Which was where they were now. She looked at her watch; almost six o'clock. Time to turn the machine back on. She worried about how they could tell for sure that the damping field was operating again. The only good test was whether or not they had contact in the night with the carnivores.

She stood up. "Let's go," she said.

This time, Ensi sensed no presence on the third floor. Silence greeted them. Only their own footfalls echoed through the immense space. The panel on the side of the machine opened as before, and she slid the control to where it had been originally. Closing her eyes, slowing her breathing, she waited. There. A faint hum. And a slight vibration in the floor. Of greater significance, her fingertips felt steady operation. Just as before. Good signs.

"What if the snake comes back during the night?" Erik asked.

"I guess we'll have to do it all over again," she answered. "Let's worry about that tomorrow. Tonight we have another problem to worry about: if someone's jamming our signals from orbit, might they not also send people down here?"

"That depends on their reason for being here, doesn't it?"

"Do you believe that it could be someone other than Walker?"

He shrugged. They had started back down the stairs.

"Who else?" he said. "I suppose there's only one way to tell."

"The companions. Yes, well, they've been concentrating on studying the inscriptions and getting through the comm barriers."

"Do you think these inscriptions match the ones on Rune-Nevas?"

"Yes. Oh, not exactly. One appears to be a later version of the other or, perhaps, a version that changed independently of the other. That they originate from the same language base is pretty clear. Which is which—which came first—we will probably never know for sure, but it would seem that these did."

They started down the last flight of stairs. Erik sneezed.

"Getting to you, too."

"Yes. Gets hard to breathe in here sometimes."

She nodded, although he could not see in the dark corridor.

"Anyway, tonight the companions are going to have to see if they can contact any strangers on the surface. I doubt that they can reach the ship up there."

"Ensi," she said silently as they stepped outside. "Are you there?"

Yes. We heard the last statement. We just tried to reach out to the racer with no success. It has to be the damper, since we can detect their presence through the jamming from above.

"Then you will have to search for strangers when the damper is off. Tomorrow. Will all of you search at once, or will only one of you be needed?"

Two of us will search. Savron will continue with analyzing the inscriptions. One of us will remain alert tonight while the other two continue with the work.

"We'll all have to be more alert now that we know someone else may be here."

I am sure that Ferguson has reached the same conclusion, Ensi said, anticipating her unspoken concern.

"Of course he has. I can't help worrying, though. They have so much to do back there."

No more than you have here.

She laughed. "Yes, a lot more. Learning the intricacies of the machine is important, but we'll be able to work at it only intermittently. That, studying the inscriptions—which is one of your tasks—and guarding against the carnivores and other intruders—well, that's it."

Ensi did not respond. Like all of them—companions and hosts alike—he found it difficult at times to separate himself from Iroshi. His work was hers, and vice versa. Of course, she would help with translating the texts as best she could. However, her ability to read the ancient language had been exaggerated.

In the early days, he had taught her enough for her to fool any experts or critics who might come along. That was when translating ancient documents hidden in the temple complex on Rune-Nevas was necessary in order to explain how she found the treasures also hidden there. The tale that was told related how she had found the documents by accident. Living there alone, she studied them with help from her background of having visited many worlds on which ancient civilizations had once thrived. That background had been the reason behind her wanderings, although she had not known it until later. She had not planned anything about it but they had: Mushimo, Ensi, and the other spirits.

Oddly, it had all been convincing. Few had questioned her ability to read the documents or her right to the treasures they revealed. Actually, she had not quite become fluent with the language. And, after twenty-three years, she had forgotten much of it through lack of usage. Reviewing the documents had never been necessary, and the demands of the Glaive had become so heavy that there had been little time for such pursuits.

When she and Erik arrived back in camp, all problems were forgotten for a time. They found Mark awake. Although weak, he was talkative and more than a little curious, especially about the dreams he had been having. They fed him some broth; then she and Erik explained about the carnivores and how they were telepathic. He asked a lot of questions, but it was soon apparent that he had no clear memories of the carnivores or their nightly forays. As he became weaker and sleepy, Erik tucked him in and Garon helped him relax. Soon he fell into a deep and untroubled sleep.

If all went as planned, he would not be disturbed for the rest of the night. Nor would they.

She perched on the highest wall of the building that had become their temporary home. Facing south, she watched the colors of the sky as the sun slipped below the hill. Surrounded by trees as it was, the view from the racer had been blocked. Maybe that was why the inhabitants of this world had built a high city. The view was spectacular and all-encompassing. If sentinels were posted on all sides, nothing could approach without being seen.

The surrounding wall at the base of the hill indicated that they had feared something. Could it have been the carnivores? If much of the old race had been telepathic, they would have needed protection against invasion of their minds, just as she, Erik, and Mark did.

However, if the race had originated here, they should have developed some inner defense. It would have been only natural if they were to survive on the same world. But they did not remain. To all appearances, there was no intelligent species still living here. Either the city builders eventually died out, or they moved on. If they were capable of leaving this world, maybe they had moved here from somewhere else in the galaxy. That meant they could also have settled on Rune-Nevas. But

Ensi's people had no record of achieving spaceflight, past or present.

A sudden flare of light made her jump. She looked around, saw Jarys lighting the lamps. Below, darkness descended gradually over the forest that stretched as far as the eye could see.

What was that, to the southeast? A column of smoke rose into the air, slightly backlit by the glow of sunset. The racer was almost due east, and she hoped they would not light an outdoor fire. Not now that they knew someone else might be on the surface. And there they were. Nothing else could explain a fire, at least as far as they had found.

Someone would have to find out, then.

"Erik," she called.

He came quietly, warned by Garon that something was up. Iroshi pointed.

"See the smoke?"

He stared in the direction indicated for a moment, then nodded.

"That's probably our friends from the orbiting ship. We'll need to find out for sure. As soon as I turn off the damper in the morning, I'll contact Ferguson and warn them. One of the companions will have to seek out our visitors. Better get the light and the fire out. Don't want them finding us just yet. We'll eat cold tonight."

"Food's ready," Erik said.

She turned and looked at their own fire. It was small, the fuel giving off little smoke: hopefully not enough for anyone down there to have seen. The glow of the fire, however, was another matter, and before they ate the fire was extinguished.

Nothing invaded her thoughts after total darkness descended. However, as she lay in her sleeping bag, her own mind kept replaying memories of earlier nights. It didn't seem possible that a sensitive race could have survived constant bombardment like that from the carnivores for any length of time. That they had caused the city's inhabitants a problem would seem to be a fact, given the existence of the damping field. Even if only a small percentage of the population had been sensitive, the need for the field would have been great. Especially if those few had been their religious leaders. However, that having been the case on Nevas would not necessarily mean it was the same here. Still, that would do as a working hypothesis.

Did the carnivores evolve and develop telepathy, forcing the city's residents to build defenses? Developing and building the damper had to take time, unless the technology already existed. Or did the people come from somewhere else among the stars, finding out too late about the animals' abilities? This city would have taken a number of years to build to this size. Generations, even. Well, whichever the case, one thing was clear, at least to her. The damper came from their need to protect themselves from the carnivores' thoughts. And in spite of the lack of any evidence, it seemed most likely that neither these people nor the carnivores originated here. If they had evolved within close proximity of each other, they probably would not have needed the damper at all.

Some protection, or perhaps even a symbiosis, would have developed naturally.

Iroshi shook her head. Any number of reasons could be behind what existed on this world.

A glance at her watch in the moonlight told her that her turn at guard was coming soon. She slipped out of the sleeping bag and stretched. If she couldn't sleep, she might as well let Jarys try. She stopped in mid-stride. A noise out on the street had caught her attention. A familiar sound.

17

✦✦✦

Graham and Andretti nearly had everything packed. For an hour's trek through the woods, they were not taking a whole lot. Just enough, Walker thought. She hefted her own rifle, then slung it over her shoulder. On a world with a safe atmosphere, she always liked to use projectile-style weapons. Laser guns had to be recharged, and it was easier to carry lots of caseless ammunition than it was to carry a recharger.

Ammunition in two packs, food and water in two others. Miscellaneous necessities in the fifth. Graham would keep the search going in other directions. Andretti and four of the men put on the packs and followed Walker.

On a foray the day before, Andretti had come across the most promising find so far: city ruins on a hill. If the racer was in the general area, chances were that the Glaivers had also found the ruins. Not a bad place to bed down, especially if the ship was ruined by the crash. Most of the buildings appeared to be in pretty bad shape, but there had to be one or two with enough walls and roof to provide shelter.

Her watch showed ten a.m. The walk back from the hill had taken Andretti just over an hour. They would have to allow that much time to return this evening. She had no intention of staying away from the camp, even in the ruins, after dark. Not after the sounds last night.

Never before had she heard such bestial noises. First the cry of fear and pain, inhuman enough to give anyone chills. Then a snap and a crunching sound, as if bones were being broken. The sound of flesh tearing followed by growls. The latter sound had been clearly a matter of dominance. That sound, although threatening, had been pleasing, reminding her how she was always trying to impress on others her own dominance. After the destruction of the head of the Glaive, she would never have to do it again.

For an hour she had lain on her cot, frightened by the sounds in spite of the electronic barrier around the camp. No animal alive on any world could penetrate that barrier. Yet she had let the fear take hold, raise the hair on the back of her neck. Her palms had felt clammy. She had held her breath for fear of being heard. Fear was a cleansing force, one that she had not felt since Duncan died. She awoke in the morning ready to take on Iroshi or anyone else who crossed her path.

Over morning coffee she, Andretti, and Graham had discussed the carnivores, whose hunting had been confirmed by scouts who found the remains of an animal in the woods.

"They must be nocturnal," Walker had said. "We heard them last night but have not seen one sign of them during the day. They shouldn't be a problem for any teams during daylight."

"Are you sure the barrier will keep them out?" Andretti had asked Graham. "Some of our people were pretty nervous this morning."

"Yes," the woman had answered. "Nothing can survive that charge, and it reaches high enough to keep anything from jumping over it."

Andretti had nodded but had not looked totally convinced. He must have been one of those made nervous. He would have to be checked out once this job was completed. For now, he led the way for their little party while Walker followed right behind him.

When the ruins came in sight, they stopped and Walker looked at her watch. One hour, twelve minutes. That meant they would have to head back before seven.

She moved up beside Andretti, and they studied the terrain together. No sign of movement or occupation.

"It's big," Andretti said. "It would take a long time to search the whole thing."

"Yes. That's why we wait here. If anyone's in there, they'll show themselves eventually. Get everyone comfortable. We watch for now."

"Yes, ma'am."

She glanced at her watch. "Jellison should have the jammer off soon." Andretti nodded. "Keep Barron on that comm. I want to know about any signal he picks up."

Andretti saluted and turned away. He set about placing each of the men where they could keep an eye on the ruins and not be seen from any direction. He instructed Barron, then took his own place just to her right. They watched and waited. No one moved a muscle, or if they did they made no noise. No one had a better mercenary force than she did. No one. Not the Glaive. Not the central council on Earth. No one.

It came about mid-afternoon. A flash of light reflecting off something metallic or possibly glass. About one-third of the way up the hill. Twice, then it was gone. She raised the binoculars. A hint of movement just before she got them focused, then nothing.

No matter. Someone was up there and playing it pretty close. Not another sign of activity the rest of the afternoon. At six-thirty, she signaled the return to camp. Tomorrow they would watch again. They would keep doing that until they had a clear picture of who was there and where they were settled.

All along she had hoped that Iroshi had been killed in the crash. Now it seemed more fitting that the two of them should meet. Hopefully, then, the head of the Glaive had been spared.

Another distress signal with the identification code of Iroshi's racer. There had been three that day. Not enough for any certainty about direction, but each time the transmission came through, there was a little more information.

The captain had asked if they should set up a continuous signal in hopes that it would get through whatever was jamming the signals. Mitchell had decided against that. If the jamming was deliberate, it might be better that those responsible not know that someone was listening out here. He regretted that this course denied any consolation to the lost crew, but doing everything to ensure their safety was much more important.

Yail had agreed not to send any reply either. At the same time, he had reported that the crew members of his ship were getting restive. They were losing a great deal of money on this rescue mission for a person they cared nothing about. The ship was a trader, and its crew had families to support back on Bosque. Some people just never saw the big picture.

The comm on his desk buzzed. It was Yail calling again.

"Mitchell, I've been thinking. My ship does not have any sophisticated equipment that's helpful in our search. At least nothing like that new triangulator you have. I think it might make better sense to send it home. I'll come aboard your ship, if that's all right with you."

"The crew still giving you trouble?"

"They're grumbling. If you can't make room for me there, I intend to make them keep up the search. However, I don't think we'll be much help in a pinch. And there are those other Glaive ships coming."

"The Glaive could offer them a reward."

Yail shook his head. "I would rather not. If they can't see how important this is, they don't deserve a reward."

They *must* have been giving him a hard time. Having the young man on board the racer did not appeal to him, but Mitchell could think of no way to refuse a berth without seeming jealous. Which he was. He had finally admitted that to himself. An unpleasant admission at best. Having Yail within an easy distance might be a constant reminder.

"Look. I know Sheera or Johnson might be of more

help to you than I can be. Maybe even Leila. But I'm not leaving until we find Iroshi."

Clearly, Yail did not intend to leave the field. He was right about the two uninjured Glaivers, but there was not enough room on his racer for all of them. Maybe the trader could rendezvous with one of the other racers and transfer them over. It was beginning to appear that the trader was more of a liability if things should come down to a fight.

"We can make room for you," he said, realizing that the long pause might imply reluctance. Let it. He owed Iroshi's young lover nothing.

The transfer was effected quickly, and the trader soon after headed back toward Bosque, in spite of protests from the Glaivers. Its captain promised to get them to a racer as soon as possible. Sheera and Johnson could make sure that he kept his word.

"We'll be better off without them," Yail muttered later as he watched the view screen, meaning the traders. He was getting the cook's tour, starting on the bridge.

"I'll show you your cabin," Mitchell said.

He led the way down the hall. The only available cabin was close to his own, one of the smallest on the ship since it was rarely used. Only in cases like this when an unexpected passenger came aboard. As they walked side by side, Yail kept casting sideways glances at him.

He must be wondering what kind of man Iroshi's longtime lover was, just as that lover wondered about the new man on the scene. Lines from William Blake came to Mitchell.

Cruelty has a human heart, and jealousy a human face; terror, the human form divine, and secrecy, the human dress.

Iroshi had introduced him to the strange poetry. Blake was one of her favorites and soon became Mitchell's. They used to sit on the bed late at night and read verses to each other. A long time ago.

Arrival at Yail's cabin curtailed more daydreaming. Mitchell opened the door and stepped aside to let its new occupant enter.

"Sorry it's so small, but it's the only empty cabin. If you need anything"—he opened a panel in the wall over the bed—"comm button, here. Emergency alarm." He flipped another, larger panel down from the wall next to the door. "Sink. The head's down the hall on the right. I'm right next door. Meals are announced with a bell. Most of us eat in the galley, but a few eat in their rooms. It's all prepared stuff."

Yail had touched the different items as Mitchell pointed out the few features. He looked the cabin over and nodded.

"It will be fine," he said. "Thanks for taking me along."

"Too bad the trader couldn't stay," Mitchell said. "Not that they had the right equipment. It would have been good for you, I guess."

Yail shrugged. "Galicia has never had military or police ships. I'd never myself considered that there might be a need one day. Maybe when I get back I should try to get funds allotted for one or two, just in case."

"It's the crews that are hard to recruit."

"I suppose. I only hope we find her and that she's all right."

The first mention of Iroshi, albeit an oblique one—the subject both were obsessed with at the moment. An awkward introduction at best.

"So do I." Mitchell clapped Yail on the shoulder. "She's pretty good at taking care of herself. And everyone with her on that racer is first class."

Yail nodded. "Uh, if there is anything I can take care of . . . I don't expect a free ride."

"We may need your skills when we find her. At the moment, there isn't much to do for anyone except the crew. I even get in the way at times."

This was getting pretty lame. Time to bow out.

"I'll leave you to settle in. Unpack. Whatever. We only ask that you keep off the bridge for the time being. Only to give the crew room to do their jobs."

"Thanks."

Mitchell backed out and closed the door. Up close and personal like that, Yail had reminded him of someone. He could not quite pull out the memory. It would come to him.

18

Iroshi.

"I hear it," she said.

As quietly as possible, Iroshi woke Erik, with a finger against his lips to caution him to be silent. The two of them joined Jarys crouched behind the front wall. She neither looked up nor said anything. All three listened intently, determining direction and distance by the sounds that continued out of the night.

Erik pointed right, then held his hand out flat, indicating that it was on the street that ran in front of their building and was coming their way. Iroshi nodded and whispered in his ear, "The snake." He nodded in turn. She whispered the same information to Jarys, whose eyes got even bigger. Erik had described the creature to her while they ate dinner.

A whine broke the night's silence, possibly the loneliest sound Iroshi had ever heard. The three exchanged glances. A pang of guilt made her look away, but she pushed the feeling back. They had no choice but to lure the creature away from the machine. Once they were able to leave this world, he could have it back.

The fact that the snake was roaming the streets was

very unsettling. However, if it had worked its way this far down the hill, it might be in the forest by tomorrow.

She motioned for Erik to move to the left while she moved right. Not a good idea for them to stay bunched up.

A dark shadow emerged at the farthest visible edge of the street. Without light to turn them red, the eyes were invisible. So was the mouth, open or not. However, just knowing about those teeth was more than a little unnerving. The entire body came into view as it scooted forward. Silently, all three of the watchers drew their guns. With a hiss, the creature stopped. It must have keen hearing.

Until it moved closer, Iroshi had to watch it through an opening in a wall of the next building. If she looked for too long, it tended to disappear against the background, fading in and out of view.

"Ensi."

I am watching it, he replied. *It is one of the most difficult creatures to detect I have ever seen.*

"Only in the dark," she said, not knowing for sure if that was true. But she had only seen it in the dark.

It started moving again, making it a little easier to see. Another whine filled the air. Was it the last of its kind? Was that why it had bonded with a piece of machinery? Difficult to believe and impossible to check under current conditions. She hoped that they would not be on this world long enough to find out. Why would anyone want to seek out more of them, anyway? One was more than enough.

From inside the building came a moan. Mark, dreaming or in pain. Whatever the case might be, the snake stopped again. Its head swung toward them, hovering just above Jarys. Erik started toward his brother. No telling what the snake would do if Mark moaned again or if it detected Erik.

"Ensi, have Savron quiet Mark if she can. And get Erik back to the wall."

In a moment, Erik slid back to his former position. The snake's attention was on the far wall, and it did not notice his movement. Jarys crouched, frozen in place. Even from seven feet away, the medic's fear was palpable. Iroshi held her breath, pressing against the wall. The snake was closer to Jarys than anyone, then next closest to Erik. However, Iroshi had a better chance than they did of hitting the thing if it struck. Or charged. Whatever it chose to do. The gun had gotten heavy enough to make her hand ache slightly, but she resisted the temptation to switch it to the left.

Her throat was suddenly very dry and she wanted to cough. She tried to swallow but had no saliva. For a moment she closed her eyes, took three deep breaths, relaxed. When she opened her eyes again, the thing had moved a little farther along the road. Suddenly it raised its head as high as it seemingly could. A howl rent the stillness. The sound went on and on, and even hands over ears could not block it. The vibrations penetrated her body. It might even have touched her heart a moment before the sound died, slowly, into a keening that bespoke mourning.

With this much agony, the thing either had not detected the restart of the machinery, or had been unable to find its way back. Whichever it might be, the creature might die of loneliness and sorrow.

Having voiced its agony, the creature moved on. Shortly it reached the end of their field of vision, its tail the last of it to disappear around the curve in the road. The three of them waited to be sure before moving or speaking.

They came together slowly, awed and shaken by the experience. A reluctance to speak still held them silent for the space of several heartbeats. There were volumes that could be said. What was most important? At last, Iroshi spoke.

"Since it's this far down the hill, it would seem that the creature is trying to find its way out of the city. There is always the chance that it could detect the machine's vibrations and try to get back to it. We'll have to keep an eye out for it at all times."

"It makes enough noise," Jarys said. "I don't think it could sneak up on us."

"Probably not," Iroshi answered. "However, we haven't seen it in a hunting mode. We don't even know if it has one. Those teeth would indicate that it's carnivorous, but . . ."

"We saw how aggressive it can be up there," Erik said into the silence. "It may not want to eat us, but it will attack in self-defense."

"Can't we just kill it?" Jarys asked.

"Not unless we have to," Iroshi said. "I would even like to get that machine operating permanently again so the snake can go back to its former way of life. This is its world. We'll need to do anything and everything to survive until we can get off-planet. However, I would like to leave it as we found it if possible."

Jarys shrugged, and Erik went to check on Mark.

"Get some sleep," Iroshi told the medic. "I'll take the watch now."

"I'll try. I don't think I can keep from listening for that thing to come back."

"As long as we keep pretty quiet for a while longer, I don't think it will come back."

Erik walked past. "I'm going back to sleep, too," he said.

"How is Mark?"

"Looks like he slept through the whole thing."

"Good. Probably the last thing he needed was to wake up face to face with a gigantic snake. Goodnight."

"Night," he said over his shoulder.

In moments, the darkness grew silent again, except for Jarys tossing in her sleeping bag and an occasional snore from Erik. Ensi was working with the other companions on the inscriptions or watching for intruders, and for the second time in days, she was almost totally alone. Solitude was something she relished, with just her own thoughts for company. However, this time her thoughts wandered to a subject she had been avoiding since leaving Galicia: Yail.

Memories of their love made fires shoot upward through her body, and she moaned. They had been tentative, as people who don't know each other well often are. There had not been enough time to learn each other's moods and flashpoints. Even so, it had been satisfying and exciting, while leaving a desire to learn more.

Was he participating in the search? Her leaving so abruptly had disappointed him so. Would he be pouting over that? She knew so little about him. She wanted to know so much more.

But there was Mitchell, too. Thoughts of him brought the familiar feelings of security and faithfulness. And love. She could not give him up, which meant she would have to give up Yail. He wanted to be a member of the Glaive, but that had to be ruled out. Having him so near, so often, would wear down her resolve. Maybe she could get him a post with the constabulary. It had been a great training ground for Mitchell and would give Yail the opportunity to travel, and to have lots of adventures. He would forget her soon.

But she did not want him to forget.

The snake was the lucky one. It knew what it wanted—no substitutes, no complications. Except, of course, that it had lost the one thing in its life. What the final outcome of that would be was difficult to say. How deep did its attachments go? How deep did her own go? What came first in her life?

The Glaive, of course. Nothing else mattered as much. Mitchell knew he was second and never minded. Or never seemed to mind. His own dedication was nearly as strong. Wasn't it? Could she have misread the dedication? They had known each other for more than twenty years, and suddenly it felt like she did not know him at all.

Which was not true. She knew him very well. When it comes to people, though, it is impossible to know everything about them. Everyone has secrets of one kind or another. Privacy. Fear. Shyness. So many different reasons for hiding feelings, thoughts, even reactions.

Ensi was as close to her as anyone could ever be to another person, yet he still surprised her once in a while. Hard to imagine life without him.

Ah, yes. When they got back to Rune-Nevas, one subject would be discussed: how to ease the pain of changing bonding partners. If they got back.

How easy it is to assume that everything will work out and all plans will be fulfilled. A person could not function if it was assumed that the worst would always happen. Especially in the darkness of early morning, when failure did not seem so remote a possibility.

Iroshi stood and stretched. Time to think more positively. Make plans. Tomorrow she would send Erik back to the ship for a few things they needed. Somewhere in her pocket there was a list . . . There. She left it where it was; easier to find in the morning.

The rest of the morning, she fought off negative thoughts, made more plans, and avoided remembering both Mitchell and Yail. Erik's snoring increased in volume, and Jarys, although asleep, still tossed and turned. Her training as a soldier made serving with the Glaive difficult for her at times. Her attitude was purely pragmatic. See a problem? Fix it. The snake was a problem. Take it out. End of problem. That she was young made her attitude firmer. As she gained age and experience, the philosophy of the Glaive would become a greater influence on her. If that did not happen, she might end up working for someone else, although people did not often leave the Glaive.

The eastern sky began to turn yellow. In a little while, Erik would make his way back to the racer and she would make her way up the hill. Another peaceful night, relatively speaking.

Jarys was not too happy about having to stay with Mark while the others went about their tasks, but she held her peace. Iroshi promised that she would be back in time for the medic to spend the afternoon exploring through some of the ruins. Erik started for the racer right after they ate breakfast. Iroshi left soon after.

The slightest noise made her start. Usually it was only the wind blowing over or through a piece of architecture; a few small animals scrabbling around in the debris. Whether they were kept away by the damper, the snake, or they simply did not exist in large numbers on this world, she still had no idea. Whatever the reason, their scarcity made the world feel a bit empty and sounds seem more mysterious.

She entered the building warily. For all she knew the snake had come back in the night and reattached itself to the machine on the third floor. Ensi searched for any signs of life in the silence.

Erik would have preferred staying with his brother and letting Jarys go back to the racer. But he had not objected, since it should be safer for him to go. And once Iroshi got the machine turned off for the day, he would be able to communicate with those in the ruins, either with the comm unit or telepathically through Savron.

Immediately after leaving the protection of the damping field, he had talked shortly with Ferguson back at the racer. The smoke that Iroshi had seen the other night made it imperative they not give away their positions any more than necessary. Even as Savron searched the immediate vicinity for traces of any other people, he moved along the trail. The smoke could have been some sort of natural phenomenon, but they could not afford to take chances. Especially now that Mark was recovering so nicely.

His brother had actually sat up and eaten a little this morning. A little more color had warmed his cheeks, although his voice was weak and his powerful physique looked slightly wasted. Hell, he was weak all over but the signs of improvement were wonderful to watch. He would probably be able to move around on his own in a day or two. The only thing they had to hope for was that the damping machine would continue working. Not that there was much chance of its quitting now, since it must have operated for centuries.

Almost too much of a coincidence that they would come this far and find evidence similar to that found on Rune-Nevas. For himself, he did not believe there was any connection at all. Only a remarkable similarity in architecture, writing, language . . .

All right. The evidence was pretty strong toward a connection, but he was not convinced. And nothing they had found explained the damn cramars, or wolves, or whatever they were called.

Ahead in the path stood a small clearing that had to be crossed or circled. Erik paused at the edge and watched for any sign of another presence among the trees. Everything looked clear, and he started to step out from cover.

The clearing shimmered as if the air had suddenly been overheated.

Erik, the carnivores, Savron warned.

Too late. It must be a dream, a reliving of the hunt while the animal slept. Movement flashed across his vision, then settled into a line straight ahead. It was all hazy, and it was earlier in the day than before. Savron tried to reach back to Ensi, but the damper was not down yet. Erik grabbed hold of the nearest tree.

The visions became distorted and disconnected. Between strong sensations, he tried to find a hiding place in which to wait until the dreams went away.

19

Walker settled into her vantage point, then looked around to make sure the others were settled. The air was still cool, and she wished that she had brought some hot coffee. It had been a pretty cool night in spite of the heat packs.

She had nixed regular fires until further notice. The hill of the ruins was high and would afford anyone— even halfway up—a clear view of much of the surrounding countryside. Smoke from a fire would have been a dead giveaway. The biggest advantage they had was surprise. The biggest disadvantage was that they had arrived at the hill this second day so late. Having to wait until there was enough daylight to travel was no good. For the next day or two, the others would remain on alert here, watching, then entering the ruins once the presence of others had been determined.

That was today's project: determine if anyone from the racer had taken up residence in the ruins and, if so, exactly where. The other squad, under Graham's leadership, was trying to locate the racer.

The sun cast shadows obliquely from her position. This entrance through the city's walls faced south. The last member of her squad watched the east gate, while the first watched the north. For whatever reason, there was no gate on the west side. Since people were prone to take the easiet path, that meant there was no reason to watch that side. Especially if those inside felt there was no reason to be extra careful, and so far there was no indication they would be on their guard.

Something rustled the undergrowth to her right. She turned, hand on pistol, but it was Barron, in charge of the comm unit.

"Graham just called," he said. "They just saw someone east of here."

"Man or woman?" Walker asked.

"Man. They're following him. Seems like he's acting very strangely."

"Andretti," she called on her hand comm. "Barron and I are going east. Graham has reported a contact there. Stay here with the rest. I'll be in touch."

"Yes, ma'am," came the reply.

"Let's go," she said to Barron.

He had gotten as specific a location as was possible within the overgrown forest, and the two of them headed confidently toward the east. Because of the height of the trees, they paused once to get their bearings. Twenty minutes out, they did a quick check with the hand comm to locate Graham. She and the squad were less than a mile ahead. Walker asked for and received no details; staying off the air was a safety precaution even though they broadcast on their own frequency. The Glaivers could be scanning all frequencies and bands.

• • •

Erik lay in thick underbrush, hands pressed against his ears. Dream sequences got through anyway, clouding his vision, overloading other senses. Logic said that covering his ears would do no good, but logic did not mean anything. Nor did Savron's voice telling him that others were near. Then the visions faded.

Erik, they are near. We must get away.

"How many?"

Ten. I think they are trying to surround us.

"You think?"

The visions affected me, too. I still feel a little unsteady.

"Tell me about it."

Erik turned onto his belly, then raised himself slowly on hands and knees. Thorns and sharp little branches pricked at his uniform, trying to pull him back down. The bushes and weeds were thick and waist-high to a standing man, the reason he had chosen to throw himself into them. Seeing him would be difficult, but so was seeing out.

Something cracked to the right and slightly behind. His heart leapt, but his head turned slowly. Quick movement was easier to detect. A shaft of sunlight piercing the stand of trees flashed off something metallic.

Then, to the left and slightly ahead, another sound of something, or someone, moving. A moment ago he was the hunter. Now he was the hunted.

"Try to reach Iroshi," he said to Savron. "She may have the damper off by now."

Not yet, the answer came a moment later. *I will keep trying.*

Erik moved his right hand to feel for the pistol at his belt. Still there. The weight of his sword on his back made it unnecessary to physically check for it.

All right. He was still armed. There were ten of them and one of him. Savron could confuse some of them. Maybe all of them. That might give him a chance to get away. He could not go to the racer. There were probably more around somewhere. Too many for the racer crew to fight off, and others might be called up. Going back to the ruins would be better, even if there were only three on their feet there. The buildings provided more hiding places than you could count, and he and Iroshi were easily a match for this many, especially with the help of the companions.

Even so, if he could get there without being followed, all the better.

A noise directly behind cut assessment short. He dropped to his stomach and rolled left, drawing the pistol at the same time. A figure with raised rifle faced him from less than five feet away. The man opened his mouth to say something. The words died when the energy bolt caught him in the throat. Before the body hit the ground, Erik was crawling, trying to bury himself deeper in vegetation. Ahead, a voice screamed; Savron working his little tricks with the mind.

A woman's voice yelled, "Get him."

Bodies crashed through the brush, some near, others farther away. Crawling was too damn slow. He rose to his knees, gripped the pistol with both hands.

Erik, right.

A figure appeared to the right. Erik fired. A cry.

Behind you.

A heavy blow against his head. Darkness threatened vision, and he tried to blink it away. Pain slammed his left temple. Another weight against his head. He fell face first into a scratchy bush.

Walker watched for the slightest sign that the man was regaining consciousness. They had returned to camp half an hour ago, and immediately she had ordered that the prisoner be placed on the ground, his back against a tree and tied to it. The ropes were tight enough to keep him sitting upright. They might even be cutting off the circulation in his extremities, which did not matter much. He would be dying as soon as he gave her the information she wanted.

Barron brought her a cup of hot coffee, then sat down on the stool next to hers.

"Sorry about Leo," Walker said.

Barron looked down at the ground. "Me, too," he said.

He and the dead man had been friends for a very long time. These mercenaries took friendship very seriously, since they trusted very few people. To them, a friend was one you could trust to watch your back, and you might find only one or two in your traditionally short lifetime.

The prisoner's head raised a little, but only for a moment.

"Looks like we might not need the stimulant after all," she said to no one in particular.

She left the small case containing the drug and syringe on the ground beside her, though. They might be useful if he was not coming around, or as a threat if he decided to pretend.

"Did you talk to Andretti?" she asked Barron without turning toward him.

"Yes. He will wait there until we contact him again."

She nodded. Once more, everything was going her way, and in a few moments, she would have the rest of the facts. Too bad, though. He was a handsome young man. Great body. He must work out regularly. He certainly looked better than any of the lovers who had come and gone since Duncan died. Three of them. No, four. Must not forget Daniel, who lasted all of three days. Not one of them compared to this. She wondered if Iroshi had ever bedded this one.

The head came up to rest against the tree trunk. The eyelids quivered, then opened. He stared at nothing a moment, then squeezed his eyes shut again.

"Headache?" she asked.

Slowly, the eyes reopened. He looked in her direction, squinting against the pain of light.

"Who . . ."

"I am Rhea Walker. And your name?"

"Erik. Everyone just calls me Erik."

He spoke slowly, seeming to drag each word out. Even though it was tinged with pain and confusion, he had a nice voice.

"Well, Erik." She stood and walked closer to him. "We need a little information, and we think you can help us with it."

"Information?"

"Yes. For instance, how many in your racer survived

the crash? Where are the survivors? Is anyone using the ruins on the hill? You know, things like that."

"I don't know . . ."

She kicked the bottom of his foot, and he winced.

"No lies. Only the truth, or things will get very ugly for you. Now . . ."

"I really don't know much. I think someone else survived, but . . ."

"We heard bits of conversation on the comm. We believe one of the voices we heard was yours."

Erik arched his back, trying to get more comfortable.

"Did you find a hand comm on me?"

She dismissed the question with a wave of her hand. "You could have lost that anywhere. Or maybe you threw it away."

"Look. I remember leaving the ship after the crash. I was hurt, and I guess pretty confused. I was looking for something—I don't remember what it was—and . . ." He looked embarrassed. "I haven't been able to find my way back."

"You got lost in the forest?"

Erik nodded.

"Bullshit!" Barron yelled.

He jumped to his feet and started toward the prisoner. Walker turned to block him, and he stopped short.

"When I need your input I will ask for it," she said as coldly as she could.

He returned to the stool, and she decided for the moment she would let him stay. The threat he presented was very real and potentially useful. As long as he stayed under control. If the questioning went nowhere, then he could take over.

"My comm man is unhappy with you," she said, turning back to Erik. "You killed his friend back there in the woods."

"He was going to kill me."

"Not necessarily. If your death was all we wanted, you wouldn't be here now. We want information."

"I can't help you."

"You will." Her palms were sweating, and she rubbed them down the front of her pants. "Now. Did Iroshi survive the crash?"

"I don't know."

She shook her head and moved back to her stool.

"You realize, of course, that we must make sure you aren't lying. It would be better if you told us everything now rather than later."

His jaw set tighter, but he said nothing. Walker motioned to Barron. He nodded grimly and took the laser pistol she held out. It was the kind generally used to clear away brush, but with an adjustable beam.

Graham stepped up to Walker.

"It would be easier if we had some of the truth serum," he said.

She shrugged. "We didn't think to bring any down. Barron will get what we need. I've seen him work before, and that time he didn't have a personal grudge."

Barron made an adjustment to the gun and fired, the beam centering on the bottom of Erik's left foot. Erik groaned and the smell of burning flesh made Walker's nostrils flare. Barron's hand and the pistol rose suddenly; the beam scorched the branches of the tree.

"What the hell are you doing?" Walker exploded.

"I didn't do it," he said. The bewildered look on his face added confirmation to his words.

"Well, who did, then?" Graham yelled.

"Wait," Walker said. "There have been rumors about the Glaive. I'll bet he's got telekinetic powers. You know. He can move things with his mind."

"If that's so, why didn't he keep us from catching him?" Barron said.

"It doesn't give them superhuman abilities," she said, giving him her most withering look. "What I have to wonder is why he let you hit his foot in the first place. He saw it coming."

Keeping a wary eye on Erik, she sat back down. If she was right, he might be able to prevent their getting information the direct way.

"We'll have to use the serum after all," she said. Turning to Barron, she said, "See if you can contact the cruiser. Have some sent down."

"No!"

"You will do as you are told," she said. "Our priority is to get the information, not provide you with amusement."

He stood with fists clenched at his sides, and she almost hoped he was going to challenge her. It was always a good idea to show everyone who was boss every once in a while. Instead, he turned and walked over to the comm setup. In a moment, he was talking to the ship, arranging the delivery. Oh, well. His backing down was as good a demonstration as anything. However, she might still have to punish him for challenging her order in the first place.

She turned from watching Barron to studying the prisoner. Erik sat with eyes closed, his chest rising and falling in rapid breathing. His left boot smoked a little from the low intensity beam Barron had used. That foot must hurt a bit.

By the time the serum arrived, another hour had passed. Waiting did not improve her temper, and she reamed out everyone who came near. That the trip down from the cruiser could not have been made any faster did not matter. In spite of her rage, she would administer the serum herself. Barron was certainly not to be trusted, and Andretti was still at the hill.

She measured the dosage carefully. She knelt down, but before administering it, she asked Erik if he might be allergic to the serum. The prisoner did not answer. He had not moved at all during the wait. In a moment it was done. His eyes remained closed, his breathing slowed.

"How long?" she asked.

"A few more minutes," Barron answered. "He's a big guy. We may need to give him a little more."

"Anything from the scouts at the hill?"

"Nothing."

"Barron, you question him when you think he's ready."

They waited a few more minutes; then he began.

"Erik, is that your true name?"

"Yes," he said in a dull voice.

"How did you come to this planet?"

"Ship crashed."

"How many survived?"

Erik said nothing.

"Erik, how many survived the crash?"

Still nothing.

"Erik, you must answer. How many survived the crash?"

Silence.

Barron placed two fingers on the pulse point in Erik's neck. After a moment he moved around to the back of the tree to check the pulse in his wrist.

"What's wrong?" Walker asked.

"He's dead," Barron said.

20

"What if they burn the body?"

Iroshi paced, anger under control, but the energy had to go somewhere. A decision had been made without consulting her, a decision that could cost Erik his life.

"What if they mutilate it?"

Iroshi, there was no time to consult. The one called Barron had already shot him once by the time we made contact. Savron . . .

"What if he can't get back? He's never gone into revay. He knows nothing about it."

Savron and I have been working with him, teaching him gradually about revay ever since Lucas's death. We did not want to be caught short again.

This was not a snap decision, then, but had been planned in a "just in case" scenario. Knowing Ensi, he had not bothered her about getting Erik—probably others, too—practicing the technique, knowing she would approve. Which, now that her temper was cooling, she did.

"Sorry, Ensi. I just feel like I've been blindsided."

She sat down, breathing deeply, nerves calming. There were still things to take care of. Rescuing Erik's body was one of them, but seeing to their own defense was of more immediate importance. Warning those still with the racer was of equal importance. Damn. Calling on the radio was not a good idea, but there was no companion to receive the warning. When Erik did not appear as scheduled, they might even send out a party to find him. Or contact her. That would give them away more than her calling would.

Or as much as the distress signal would. They should be sending on a regular basis. Walker's party might be able to home in on that just as easily, depending on how they were scanning. The distress call left the racer in a narrow band, widening as it left the planet's atmosphere. In space the widening had to be programmed for a certain distance.

Better that she call. As long as Ferguson did not respond, and he shut down the distress signal, they would not give themselves away. However, her position, and the fact that there were two separate groups, would be revealed.

"Ensi, can you think of any good hiding place in the university? Mark is still weak, and Jarys and I can't hold off a large force by ourselves."

What if Ferguson and the others come?

"No, they must not. They might be ambushed on the way. And there are only three of them. They couldn't increase our chances against twenty or more."

"Iroshi," Mark called.

She went to his side. The improvement in his appearance since yesterday was striking, and it was clear that his strength was returning. He was still weak, though, but concern for his brother had made him determined to get on his feet. Restraining him had taken every bit of her and Jarys's strength. Once more, he was trying to get up.

"Mark, you're still too weak," she said, placing a hand on his chest. "Your brother would never forgive us if we let you get hurt again."

He lay back down but did not relax. All he knew at the moment was that Erik had been captured. If he knew about the torture and revay, he would not be convinced so easily.

"For now, we have to find a place of safety," she continued. "Before we do that, we'll have to get word to Ferguson."

"That could bring them here," Jarys said from behind.

The medic had been busy packing up. She had questioned how Iroshi could know that Erik had been captured. She was young and new to the Glaive. Before long, she would accept that the members often knew things in ways she would never understand.

"Better here than to the ship. We know for sure that they're dirtside and looking for us. Ferguson and his crew don't. They wouldn't know until it was too late."

She smiled at Jarys and put a reassuring hand on Mark's shoulder.

"Get ready to move. Both of you. I'll warn Ferguson."

She stepped into the street and lifted her face to the sun. Its warmth touched the skin but had no effect on the chill that spread inside. Turning back, she saw Jarys hand Mark a bag for him to pack with items she put beside him. Good to keep him busy.

She keyed the hand comm, and in a moment Ferguson

answered. Okay, the jamming had not been resumed from the ship.

"Don't say anything else," Iroshi warned. He remained silent. She described the situation as quickly as possible. "Shut down the distress signal," she went on. "No outgoing communication from the racer."

Quickly she went on to explain about Rhea Walker's presence on the planet and that she and her people had captured Erik.

"I suggest you might want to leave the racer and find a place to hide in the forest. Take with you everything you can load in a hurry. Particularly weapons and food. I am aware that they may be monitoring this transmission and will offer no further advice."

She stopped a moment. Was there anything else that needed to be said?

Break off soon, Ensi warned.

"Good luck," she finished. Now nothing was left to be said.

She helped finish packing. Two bags contained items they could do without for a while, and she stuffed them into holes in the back walls. She and Jarys put on their packs and started to place the other bags on Mark's litter. He sat up and swung his legs over the side.

"Where do you think you're going?" Iroshi asked.

"I'm walking." Before she could protest, he went on. "Look, the two of you can't carry the packs, the bags, and me all the way up this hill. I don't know if I can make it on my own, but I can try."

"No," she said. "We'll make two trips if we have to."

"One trip is better. They could be here any moment."

He is right, Ensi said. *Those surrounding the hill await the rest who are preparing to move this way. They overheard you and no longer feel the need for information from Erik.*

"They think he's dead, anyway," Iroshi said. "How long will it take for them to get here?"

Perhaps two hours to the base of the hill. A little more. It is a long way up that hill, even from here, and we will need time to find a hiding place.

"All right," she said aloud. "Let's go. And, Mark, the moment you feel that you can go no farther, let us know. Don't play hero. We don't have time for that."

He nodded. Picking up one of the tent poles, she handed it to him.

"Use this as a cane," she said.

He smiled and thanked her, and she led them out into the street. She set the pace up the hill, not as fast as she would have liked. Jarys brought up the rear with the powered litter and its load. Part of her task was to watch Mark. Occasionally Iroshi moved ahead, stopping to survey the streets below and the outermost wall. When the other two caught up, she set the pace for them a little, then raced ahead again.

"How close?" she asked Ensi after the third time.

They are almost within sight of the hill, he reported. *If we do not hurry, they will be able to see us soon.*

She gauged the distance to the entrance of the university. About another fifteen or twenty minutes at their present pace.

"How many?"

Twenty or twenty-five.

"Are they headed for the east entrance or one of the others?"

Their plan is to split up and come in through the east and south entrances.

"We have to hurry, then."

She went back to Mark, whose face had turned red with his exertions. His breathing was rapid, and he was drenched with sweat.

"Sorry, Mark, but we have to hurry. They're coming."

He nodded and helped make room on the litter. With the extra load, the motor labored even more as it climbed. Iroshi grabbed the frame on the front and started pulling as Jarys pushed from behind.

"Damn," Mark muttered over and over.

When she had more breath, Iroshi planned to tell him that his walking part of the way had saved the litter that otherwise would have burnt out. Heavy-duty though it was, that steep a hill was too much for it.

Right now they had to get inside the building and out of sight. They would have to find a hiding place on the first floor. Mark could not possibly climb both flights of stairs, and the litter motor would give out at any moment.

The climb was nearly over—the dark doorway yawned just ahead.

Get down! Ensi warned. *They are within sight of the hill.*

She dropped to the roadway, motioning for Jarys to do the same. They got the litter lowered. Between them and the doorway lay open space. The best they could do was to get close to the buildings on the right side and hope they would blend in enough. She looked down at her maroon uniform, partly covered with dust.

"Rub dirt on your uniform," she told Jarys, then followed her own instructions.

The medic worked on her dark blue uniform; then the two of them scattered more of the light tan dust on each other's backs. When they were done, they worked on Mark's. From a distance they might blend in with the surroundings.

"Against the wall," she said in a low voice, while motioning to the right. Speaking softly was instinctive, and knowing the enemy was too far away to hear did not matter.

They edged forward to the last corner of the last building. The litter motor coughed and stopped.

They have not seen us, Ensi reported.

All that was left was the width of the street in front of the university and the porch. She and Jarys would have to crawl and drag the litter between them.

Walker followed Graham through the east gate. Four mercenaries were already inside and had signaled that it was safe for them to enter. Those entering on the south side, led by Andretti, were to start searching the bottom street encircling the hill. Walker and her group were taking the second street. In a maze of buildings like this, the best plan was a street-by-street, house-by-house search. There must be hundreds of places to hide in such ruins.

A heavy discussion had gone on while they observed the ruins about how they should proceed once inside. Andretti had wanted to lead his group right to the top, occupying that most prominent building sitting almost intact. He had proposed working his way down to Walker's group, thus squeezing the Glaivers between them. However, Walker nixed that proposal.

"We only number twenty-five," she had said. "If we split up like that, we'll be spread too thin to keep anyone from slipping by us."

"But we have four outside observers, watching for any movement other than our own," he argued. "One or two of us can get to any site much faster. It would take less time to flush them out."

"I want to be absolutely sure that we don't miss them. We could lose the comms again like we did last night. If that happens, they could slip out without even the perimeter guards seeing them."

He had started to argue further, but she shook her head and he said nothing more. Neither plan could guarantee success, but she felt that hers was more certain.

Even so, the search would be frustratingly tedious and stressful. Remaining at the base of the hill in a base camp had its appeal, but that, too, she had decided against. Better to keep busy and not take a chance on missing the action.

If Iroshi was here, this was one kill Walker wanted to be in on. The Glaive bitch must know who and why.

Mark did not protest as he and the litter were shoved into a blind corner of a side room. He was visibly exhausted, but Iroshi hoped he was strong enough to keep a lookout for himself. She and Jarys had to find a better hiding place.

"Look down that main corridor," Iroshi instructed, pointing at the black maw. "There are several rooms on both sides. I'll look through these. It would be nice if we could find a secret panel of some kind. Of course, if we can find it, so can they." She muttered the last statement to herself. "If anyone comes in, I'll send you a message, a silent one."

Jarys looked puzzled, but only nodded and disappeared down the corridor.

You are assuming that she can pick up a message, Ensi commented.

"You'll just have to make sure that she does. We can't afford to fire a warning shot."

True enough. I have been thinking.

"Yes?" she prompted as he hesitated. She had entered another side room as empty as the first one except for fallen stones and smaller debris. Their first cursory inspection had shown no unusual features, especially anything that might help them now.

What about the elevators?

"What do you mean?"

What if we could get on top of one of the cars?

She left the room, went to the next.

"Even if we could lift ourselves *and* Mark on top, there are no guarantees that the cables, or whatever they moved on, would hold. We don't even know if there *are* any cars in those shafts."

Let us look.

"What do you suggest we use to pry the door open with?"

We never did try to open them, did we? They might not be as tough as we thought.

"Do you know something about them that I don't?" It would not be the first time in their relationship.

He almost sighed. *Do you remember the hinges on the doors in the temple on Rune-Nevas?*

"Yes."

They were still working when you opened that door from the water chamber. The metal was uncorroded and as strong as the day the hinges were made. If this civilization had the same technology we had, their elevator cables might be made of the same alloy. Our Nevan descendants used it.

"I don't know, Ensi. It seems like a real long shot."

You have the ability in your hands to check. The way they sense weaknesses in manufactured parts.

"I used to. I haven't done anything like that in years."

You did it with the machine upstairs. Try. It is the best chance we have.

"And if we spend time on this and find we can't use the elevators, what then?"

There are not many options.

She checked her watch. "We have to get the damper turned back on in five hours. Six at most."

Ensi said nothing. If he was right about the plan the invaders were following, none of them would reach the university before dark. However, if reinforcements came, they might change that plan. She had been standing in an empty room, immersed in the conversation. She stepped into the rotunda.

"Get Jarys," she instructed aloud.

The sound echoed back from the dome above and the walls around her. At the moment, Walker and her people were too far away to hear.

The sounds of Jarys's return scratched through the corridor into the rotunda. As she made her way back, Iroshi went to look through their few possessions for something to use as a pry bar. Mark offered one of his swords, but she refused, not wanting to take a chance on breaking the blade, no matter how small a chance that might be. She thought she had seen . . . Yes, there it was. A short metal bar, tapered at one end, that Ferguson had added, saying something about locked doors. She had almost refused, thinking it both unnecessary and heavy to carry. As she hefted it, she was not only grateful to the captain, she also realized that it was lighter in weight than it looked.

That was the good news. The bad news was the rod was only about two feet long. It might not give enough leverage.

"What's the plan?" Jarys asked from behind.

"One of the elevators. First we have to pry open the door so we can get to the car and see if it's stable."

Iroshi raised the bar.

"Oh, I didn't know we brought one of those," Jarys said. "Strong little sucker."

She held out her hand, and Iroshi passed it over. With one hand on each end, she suddenly extended the rod to twice its length.

"How did you do that?" Iroshi asked.

Jarys looked a little smug. "There's a pressure pad right here." She pointed to the spot. "Press here, pull here"—she took hold of the other end—"and . . ." She pushed it back together. "Even though the one end is smaller, none of the tensile strength is lost. This thing won't bend under any pressure we can apply."

"Let's go, then."

They started with the nearer elevator to the left of the main entrance. The door fit so close to the side wall that it took minutes just to wedge the tapered end of the rod between them. First Iroshi tried, then Jarys. On her second try, Iroshi finally got a purchase that widened as she rocked the rod back and forth. The two of them grabbed it, one pushing and the other pulling, until the door had opened several inches. They could not hold it, though, and, as carefully as possible, they let the door shut against the pry bar.

"We'll need some stones to prop it open," Iroshi said between panting breaths. "That thing still has a good spring mechanism of some kind."

Jarys nodded, unable to speak. When they caught their breath, they gathered up several large stones from various rooms. They placed one right next to the edge of the door and worked to open it again. With enough clearance, Iroshi pushed the stone between the door and wall with her foot, careful not to push it too far. As near as she could tell from the small opening, the car was not on this floor. She shone the torch through, but the opening just was not large enough to be sure.

"One more," she said.

This time they laid the pry bar aside and pushed and pulled with their hands. The door moved grudgingly but silently. After the passage of so many centuries, one would think the mechanism would squeal or make some kind of noise.

A second rock was placed beside the first. A third. She used the torch again. Okay. The car was in the basement. The cables lay on its roof. With this one, they would have to get everything down one flight of stairs. A little easier for Mark than going up.

The two women sat on the floor, Jarys leaning against the door, Iroshi against the wall. In spite of almost daily exercise with the swords, Iroshi felt out of shape. Was it age, or sitting on her ass too much back at headquarters? Or both? She needed to get in the field more often, or she would never be able to recover her old strength.

Check the other one, Ensi said.

"This is taking too long," she replied silently. "Where are Walker and her people?"

They are just finishing up on the first street. I doubt they will reach the top until tomorrow.

"How long until sunset?"

Five hours.

"We need to be settled in four. I'm going down to check out the basement. If the elevator door is closed there, too, we'll have to decide which is quicker—lowering ourselves from here or getting the other door open."

You are not going to try the other elevator?

"I just don't think we have enough time." To Jarys she said, "I'm going downstairs to check out the elevator door there. Stay here in case I need some information on what you can see from here."

Jarys nodded. Iroshi trotted down the corridor, the

torch beam bouncing side to side. She paused only a moment at the stairway. On the third floor they had found a gigantic, toothed worm. What might be waiting below?

Like the stairs leading up, these spiraled, limiting the space lit by the torch. Although time was limited, she must go slowly, being sure of her footing, checking ahead as much as she could. This part of the staircase was longer than a single floor upward. She reached the bottom and had seen nothing to worry about. Mostly dust that had not been disturbed in years.

The darkness was complete, unlike the upper floors where some small light got in from the broken roof of the rotunda. If something happened to the torch . . . She gripped it tighter as she exited into an identical corridor that led into a space corresponding to the rotunda on the first floor. Heavier debris littered the floor, although the walls seemed solid enough. Both elevator doors were closed. She tried the left one. Closed tight. It would take just as much work to get it open down here as it had above.

"Jarys," she hollered. "Can you hear me?"

No answer.

She pulled the katana from the scabbard on her back and banged on the door. In a moment an answering knock filled the shaft on the other side. Clearly heard, and that meant they would have to be very quiet once in the elevator.

This was as good a hiding place as any. Both doors were shut tight, making it difficult for Walker to get at them. One problem: little chance of these acting as a back door for them. There might be some way within the shaft to climb up to one of the higher floors, possibly even maintenance access of some sort. Better check it out.

She went back to the first floor. Once out of the greater darkness, she tried to relax a little. Until then, she had ignored the tension. Action could sometimes make it possible to ignore phobias, until that action was complete. Her hand shook as she replaced the sword.

"We don't have to worry about the soundness of the cables," she said silently to Ensi. She hurried along the corridor toward the rotunda.

True, Ensi said. *You will have to make sure about a ladder or some means of gaining access to the upper floors.*

She strode toward the elevator doors. Jarys watched her expectantly.

"The doors are shut tight down there, too," Iroshi said aloud. "We'll lower ourselves from here." She glanced at the outer doorway. "Anything from our friends?"

"I caught a glimpse of someone when I looked out once. But way down the hill."

"Good," Iroshi said. "Get the rope. I'm going down the shaft to take a look." Jarys held up the coil, then began pulling the end free. One step ahead. Good. However, she started to tie the end around herself.

"No, Jarys. I'm going down."

"You take too many chances, Iroshi. If you don't mind my saying so."

"I don't mind, but there are reasons why I must do this myself."

Jarys shrugged and stretched out the rest of the rope.

Iroshi saw to the few preparations necessary: tying the rope around her waist and fastening the torch to her wrist being the most important two. Except for her presumed ability to know the strength of metal and machinery, there was no real reason she had to do this herself. However, once Ensi had reminded her, she wanted to confirm that the talent was still there.

Meanwhile, Jarys measured out the rope and tied it around one of the room doors.

"I don't know how well that will hold," she said. "It seems strong enough. I'll feed the rope out to let you down."

Iroshi nodded and stepped to the opening into the shaft. Jarys braced her feet—one against the wall, the other against the door. Iroshi backed toward the edge, then stepped over the stones holding the door open, careful not to knock any of them out of place. It took only a moment to establish a rhythm as she rappelled down the smooth wall. Occasionally she pointed the torch down to see how close the roof of the car was.

"I'm there," she shouted when her feet came to rest on the horizontal surface. "Give me some slack."

The rope played out, then stopped. Jarys's face and head appeared above. With that point of reference, the distance was about forty feet, somewhat more than it had seemed from above.

"Brace yourself," she hollered. Jarys's face disappeared.

Grasping the rope with both hands, she jumped up and down on the car. It did not budge. Good. Now, how to get inside? It took several minutes to find the outline of a hatch in the smooth metal surface. She moved the cables to one side and in another few minutes had found the magnetic catch along one edge. The hatch popped up with a high-pitched squeal. About four feet square, the opening was large enough for everything they had with them.

Lying flat, Iroshi shone the torch inside. The car looked clear except for a layer of dust on everything. Its inside size looked to be about eight by eight feet. Dull metal walls reflected little light back; a control panel was set into the wall next to the door.

"More slack," she yelled. "I'm going inside."

She swallowed hard. Like hell she was going inside! She should have let Jarys do this.

Iroshi, you have done this before, Ensi reminded.

"It's been a long time," she said.

Just take a deep breath. He droned on, encouraging, supporting, pushing.

She turned to let her feet down through the opening. She shone the torch downward, gauged the distance, and dropped through. The floor caught her a little more quickly than she expected, and she fell to her knees. Dust scattered into the air all around her, and she sneezed.

Okay. The car was solid; it had not even trembled when she landed. Nothing lived inside that would be a threat to the three of them. And, once she was inside, her claustrophobia was not as bad as she had expected it would be. They would have to leave the hatch open in any case.

All right, then. Get back up on top and see about a way up from here.

She jumped up, grabbed the edges of the opening eight feet above the floor, and pulled herself through. Back on the roof, she shouted for Jarys to be ready to start pulling. The rope tightened slightly, and the medic's head appeared again in the door opening.

Examining the cable, Iroshi found that it simply hooked into a ring on top of the car. It had nothing to do with lowering or raising the car, only acting as a brace in case something went wrong. There was nothing on the roof to indicate how the car operated. However, on all four sides, between the walls of the shaft and the walls of the car, were panels with a tongue-and-groove configuration.

She studied them a moment, but could only guess at how the setup operated. It appeared that a vacuum had been created that drew the car in the desired direction. Placing her hands on one panel, she let them and her fingers feel along its length. Maybe it had been a magnetic field. However it had functioned, nothing worked now, locking the car permanently in place where it was.

Okay. What else? Ah, there it was: a ladder bolted to the wall, probably for maintenance purposes. However, it was not on the same wall as the door, and it was slightly recessed. That would explain why it had been invisible from the doorway. It did seem odd that the position of the ladder made it difficult to reach from the door, which would give easier access to anyone having to climb up or down the shaft. It might mean there were maintenance access doorways opening into the shaft. If so, they would be difficult to find and, hopefully, would not be any easier for Walker and her crew.

Iroshi undid the rope from around her waist and yelled for Jarys to pull it up. She climbed up the ladder. At the first-floor level, she discovered a narrow ledge running from the ladder to the door. In another moment she was back in the rotunda.

"We'll have to lower Mark and most of what we brought with the rope," she said. "We had better get started."

They let Mark down first. He protested that he was strong enough to use the ladder but shut up once Iroshi told him that was not an option. He stayed on the roof to control the equipment and supplies as they were lowered. Once the heaviest items were in the shaft, Jarys and Mark worked at lowering everything else into the car, and Iroshi started up the shaft to the upper floors. That path might be their only escape route if they were somehow discovered. She would also have to get to the third floor to turn on the damper before the sun set.

The climb was tiring but not difficult, and she stopped at the third floor. However, with the doors closed on the other floors, there was nowhere to go once she got that high. There had to be an easier way to exit the shaft.

Use your hands, Ensi said. *You do have the ability. If there is an opening in the walls, you can find it.*

No reason not to. They had worked with the damping machine and maybe with the elevator. She tightened her grip with her left hand on the ladder and placed her right against the wall on that side. Back and forth. With all other openings being square or rectangular, this one—if it existed at all—would probably be the same basic shape. Leaning out, she reached as far as she could. Nothing. It was hard not to be disappointed.

Try closer to the ladder, Ensi said.

"Do you know something I don't? Is this familiar to you?"

Possibly.

Starting at the edge of the depression for the ladder, Iroshi ran her fingers up and down. Then along the inside edge of the depression. There! Something . . .

A touch plate so much a part of the wall that the torch showed no features when shone fully onto it. She pressed it every conceivable way, but nothing happened. Taking a deep breath, she concentrated on the sensation of fingertips against metal. Sense the age of its making. Feel its weakness and strength. Press . . . here.

The section of ladder suddenly slid right with a sigh. A three-by-six-foot section of the depressed wall was a panel that swiveled inward. The light of the torch revealed a short, narrow passage but no other opening. If it led to another opening in the wall on the third floor, the passage must turn right.

Below, Jarys and Mark had probably gotten everything they could down into the car. She should get back and help with the heavier things, including Mark. She felt close to overload and preferred anything to entering the black passage that yawned in front of her. However, access to the third floor must be found. Better sooner than later.

Gingerly she took one foot from the ladder and set it on the floor of the passageway. Solid. Second foot. Let

go of the ladder. That took a little longer. The beam of
light from the torch shone on a wall four feet ahead.
Three steps forward, and it revealed a turn to the right.
Another wall five feet from there that must open into the
third floor. Again, no visible opening.

She took the few steps to the end and began feeling
for another touch pad. Now that she knew what it was
and how it felt, finding it took less time than for the first
one. The wall in front of her slid aside.

A hiss, and fetid breath blew in her face. The torch
light reflected off sharp, white teeth in gaping jaws. She
slammed the touch pad and jumped back. The door slid
shut, and the snake slammed against it three times before silence came once more.

Iroshi started breathing again. She wiped sweat from
her eyes. The monster had returned in spite of the
damper being turned off. Maybe it had sensed the vibrations last night. A definite problem for later.

*Sorry, Iroshi. I never sensed the thing was there. I
was concentrating on Walker and her band.*

"It's all right, Ensi. We should have had Savron keeping us posted on Walker."

*If only the monster had a stronger presence. Then I
would have sensed it anyway.*

"I know. This thing's lack of brainpower makes it
more dangerous than many intelligent beasts."

Her knees buckled slightly, and she slid down the
wall to a sitting position. Her heart beat so loudly . . .

Delayed reaction. The thing's return complicated matters considerably. Deal with it this evening. For now, go

back down and make sure both Mark and Jarys were safely placed in the elevator car.

A little later, she stood on the elevator roof, relieved to be out of the narrower tunnel. The two had managed to get almost everything lowered into the car. Mark was stretched out on top of the elevator. Jarys sat calmly beside the doors, waiting for Iroshi's return. A look of relief slid across her face.

"Hi, Mom, I'm home," Iroshi said. Jarys grinned. "Let's get you down there. I need for you to turn on the lamp so I can see if any of the light shows out here."

Jarys lowered herself to the car, then dropped inside. She pushed up the hatch door, and it squealed shut. Iroshi turned off her torch. Black as a moonless night on Rune-Nevas. Even so, they should probably keep the lights off if—or when—Walker and company got into the building.

She and Jarys then rigged up a rope to open the hatch and to use in climbing out. The pry bar was long enough to push it closed from the inside. They lowered Mark inside, and he curled up in a corner and went to sleep in spite of himself.

"See if you can make him some more room," Iroshi told Jarys. "Try to get all the gear organized a little better so we'll have some room to lie down, too. I'll be back down in a bit."

Jarys nodded. From the looks of her, it wouldn't be long before she fell asleep, too. The day had been pretty long for all of them, and she felt in need of rest herself. But not yet. Two things left to do.

After reclosing the hatch, Iroshi climbed up the ladder to the rotunda. She located the touch pad that opened the access door. This one worked, too, although with a squeal rather than a sigh. In case of emergencies only. She closed it back, then stepped out of the shaft and to the door leading outside. Twilight was not far off, and Ensi had reported that Walker was settling her people into a cold camp for the night. He indicated the buildings they had selected, but there was no visible sign of occupation. Nor was it a good idea for her to stay in the open much longer.

"Ensi, remember that night in the temple when you introduced me to ghosts?"

Yes.

Of course he did. He had used them again in Galicia.

"Let's give them a taste of haunting. Enough to keep them awake all night."

It will be my pleasure.

"I knew it would be."

Oh, on second thought, I will let Savron have the pleasure of beginning. You have to go back up on the third floor. I will need all of my concentration to try to locate the snake. After that, we can both work on our friends down there.

She went back to the elevator door. Placing her back against the door, she braced a foot against the wall to hold the door open. With her other foot, she pushed the stones clear, then squeezed out of the way to let the door close. The spring was still good enough to keep the door from slamming. Instead it slid to with only a slight scraping noise.

With a spare shirt that she had kept out of their gear, she brushed the dust on the floor in front of the elevator, trying to make it look even. Moving backward, she continued brushing until she had reached the center of the rotunda.

"They may make so many bootprints they won't see ours," she said to herself. If time permitted, there was more dust in the side rooms that could be spread on top. Anything to make the floor look undisturbed in front of the elevator door.

You had better get upstairs, Ensi reminded her.

Iroshi nodded and made for the staircase at the end of the corridor. Passing the second floor, she drew the sword from the scabbard draped across her back. It made a sound similar to the snake's hiss, and a shudder passed through her. Where was the thing now?

On the third floor, she moved more quickly and quietly toward the damper. The fetid odor of the worm's breath hung in the air, but not as strong as it would have if the creature were near. Ensi sensed its presence, but it seemed to be at a great distance. Which, of course, told them little, since he could not sense it up close sometimes.

As quickly as she could, Iroshi turned the machine on. She and Mark were now protected from the minds of the carnivores. What of Erik? No word had come for several hours—Garon was concentrating on helping him adjust to his new situation. But he would have to return to his body soon, or death might be permanent. Either way, the torments of the hunt would assail him with full force, and in his present disembodied condition he might be more vulnerable.

Hurriedly she went back to the second floor and located the access door. Sheathing the sword, she entered, found the ladder and descended to the elevator car. One more escape from the toothed beast. Time for Ensi to join Savron in entertaining the other city occupants.

21

The frustration level had been about as expected. Nothing found so far except footprints in the dirt leading everywhere and nowhere. More than one person had been in the ruins recently, exploring the streets and remains of the buildings.

Walker took off her right boot and started rubbing her foot. The left, already freed, did not ache quite as much as the right. Her companions went about their tasks rather more quietly than usual. The ruins had spooked a few of them a little; warriors' superstitions, she supposed. They had a few, including an uneasiness about long-dead places. If bodies littered the ground and the smell of gunfire filled the air, that would not bother them. Here, no bodies, and the only smell was dust and long disuse.

One more day—that was all it would take to ferret out whoever was here. They had searched more than half the ruins. As the day had progressed, the building on the crest of the hill had become more and more fascinating. They would enter it tomorrow no matter their progress.

"Walker," Barron called from the comm setup.

"What is it?"

"We've lost communication again. About ten minutes ago."

"Complete loss?"

"Yes. We can't get the cruiser or the base camp."

She tried her hand comm but got only static. All communication blocked near sunset, the same as last night. It could not be a natural phenomenon. Were the Glaivers doing it, then? That did not seem likely, since they were still unable to send out even a distress signal.

"Andretti, send out a couple of people," she ordered. "See if we can reach each other here in the ruins. If so, see how far."

"Right."

"Barron, see about getting some more lamps lit. No need in hiding our presence. Set lookouts within sight of one another completely around the hill. We don't want anyone slipping through during the night. Each one with a lamp."

And to let their quarry know they were surrounded. If the Glaivers got nervous, so much the better.

Walker settled back against the half wall where her sleeping bag was spread out. Cooking smells wafted toward her on the slight breeze that had picked up. Her eyes closed. She was tired—a good kind of tired, physical rather than emotional; good for sleep.

She opened her eyes and started. A figure stood in front of her, shadowed with its back to the lamps. Even like that, it was clear that he was not one of the mercenaries: the outline was wrong, the posture was threatening.

"Rhea, you have disappointed me again," an all too familiar voice said.

"I'm sorry, Duncan," she said while the stones behind blocked any escape.

A voice yelled nearby, but it had nothing to do with her. What had she done to anger her husband this time? How could she anger someone who was dead?

"Rhea, you will have to be punished."

"No. Please."

He wasn't real! She pushed sideways into a corner. The figure turned, keeping her under his eye and himself in shadow.

"Go away," she screamed. "You're dead. You can't hurt me anymore."

A scuffle of some kind was going on, but she could not focus on anything beyond the figure of her husband. He took two steps toward her. The stones would not give way.

"Stand up and take your punishment like an adult."

"I didn't mean to do it."

"It's too late to apologize. No way to make amends. I'm sorry, Rhea, but you have to learn."

Her hand searched the wall for an opening while she kept her eyes on Duncan. Maybe at the bottom, near the floor. Trembling fingers closed on cold metal. The butt of her pistol sticking out of the holster at her waist. This time he would not touch her. She could fight back.

"Leave it there," he ordered.

She clutched at the gun, found the safety strap and pulled it loose. He smiled. His face was still shadowed, but . . . he smiled. In the same way. He had always controlled her, knew she would never willingly disobey.

The pistol slid free of the holster, its weight reassuring. She raised the gun and pointed.

"You can't shoot me."

She fired. He stumbled backward, clutching at his abdomen. His legs gave way and he fell to his knees.

"*You* killed me again," he said, pain edging his voice.

He fell face forward into the dirt. Acrid smoke rose from the gun barrel, stinging her nose and eyes. Tears welled up, and she turned to lean on the wall.

She killed him. How could she do that? He would be so angry.

No, you fool. He's dead. Been dead. You killed him just like before.

She turned back around. The body was gone. Tentatively, she stepped away from the wall. Where could he have gone? In the distance, her mercenaries fired at an enemy hidden in the night. They needed her.

Before she could join them, Andretti yelled, "They're gone."

The firing gradually subsided.

"Did you get a good look at them?" she asked him as she ran up.

"No. Just a glimpse of them in the darkness."

"What did they look like? Did anyone see them?"

She turned to the others as they started to gather around. One described a couple of soldiers in the uniforms of the Earth Force. Another saw a civilian dressed as a miner. Still another saw a man in a kilt wielding a sword.

"This is crazy," Walker said. "I saw someone . . . something entirely different. Did any of you recognize a face? Someone you might know?"

They all shook their heads.

"Maybe they were the ghosts of the people who used to live here," a voice said. Someone laughed, and others shifted their feet as if they might have been thinking that very thing and were glad they were not the ones caught at it.

"Nonsense," Walker said. "The whole thing was something the Glaivers rigged up. Holograms or something." She turned to Andretti. "Send someone out to check with each of the guards around the hill. Make sure no one has left his post. Everyone stay alert in case there's another attack."

Andretti drew close. "We might send two to check on the guards. They're all pretty nervous."

"Okay. Just get them going."

He nodded and left her. In a few minutes, two men left the lamplit area. One of them carried a lamp along with his rifle rather than a torch. Just as well; it would not only help their nerves, it could also give them a clearer view of their surroundings. Those left in the camp went about their tasks a little more loudly than they should have.

This whole incident smacked of magic. Whatever the cause, the source was the Glaivers. She was sure of that much. How they could create such powerful illusions was a mystery she intended to investigate. Such a talent would come in handy.

From a distance came a sound that she could not quite make out.

"Quiet!" she ordered.

That was gunfire.

Andretti came near again. "Sounds like the other side of the hill," he said. "Do you want to send a patrol to check it?"

The firing stopped. They waited, listening until their minds created sounds.

Walker shook her head. "I have the feeling we might be sending people out all night at this rate. Once those two you sent out get all the way around, maybe they'll all understand that these are illusions. Make sure everyone here in camp knows that. I don't want them out there shooting at everything that moves."

Firing started up toward the south. They looked at each other.

"Better send a couple back to base camp in the morning," she said. "We'll probably need more ammo."

He nodded with a lopsided grin, then shook his head as more shots were fired a little closer.

"It's going to be a noisy night," he said.

"Yes, so it would seem."

She returned to her sleeping bag and lay down. Immediately thoughts of Duncan came to torment her. The things he had said when he appeared. No one could know about that. She had not told a soul, nor had he. She had even convinced herself of his suicide. The last thing he had ever wanted was for anyone to know how he treated his wife or that she had killed him. Theirs was supposed to be the perfect marriage, always in harmony, the best little wife a man could ask for. And she? She wanted nothing more than to please her husband, be the best helpmate he could ever ask for. Pretty old-fashioned to a lot of people, but that was how marriages were where he came from. Or how they appeared.

She had met his mother once. Hard to forget that look in the woman's eyes, dull, kind of lost, hopeless. Those eyes had looked back at her one other time: when she looked in the mirror at herself. It was a long time before she looked that close again. Not until months after Duncan had died. The look had gone, replaced by one of determination, even hatred. Aimed at the Glaive.

Gunfire erupted around her. Leaping to her feet, she grabbed her own pistol. Damn, it was going to be a long night.

"The signals stopped again," Mitchell said. "However, we got a near fix on the source. We'll be jumping at the next coordinates, which will get us into the right sector."

"How close does that put us?" Yail asked.

"This particular sector is mostly unexplored," Mitchell said. "What little information we have indicates that there are several hundred planetary systems. None are supposed to be inhabited. Either by colonials or indigenous species."

"Several hundred? The only hope we have, then, is for the signal to come again." Yail thought a moment. "So far, the signal has come at specific hours, for just as specific a length of time. It has to come tomorrow at the same time as before."

He was right, of course. If the signal did not repeat, locating the right planet would be nigh impossible.

They talked a while longer about the different courses of action open to them. Doing a sensor sweep of hundreds of planets was a possibility, and they came up with no way to make it faster if there was no further signal. Exhaust residue had more than likely dispersed by now; none had been detected up to this point.

They talked it all out, nothing was left to say, and they sat in silence several minutes. Yail looked up from studying his hands resting on the tabletop between them.

"Guess I'll get to bed," he said. "Or read or something."

Mitchell nodded, and they said goodnight. He had found that he was glad of the younger man's company in a perverse sort of way. That he cared for Iroshi was evident in every word he said, and having someone who understood his own personal concerns actually helped. It should have made him jealous; it did at first. But jealousy gave way to sharing. They had avoided talking about their relationships with her. Thank goodness. Instead, they had talked about her role as head of the Glaive and her skills as a warrior. Yail had seen her in action once. Mitchell had seen her several times. Both agreed that it was something to see.

Yail probably had not guessed that Mitchell knew he had been her lover. How could he know?

Regardless of all that, he could not bring himself to consider the possibility of sharing Iroshi's affections. He was old-fashioned in that regard, yes, but more than that, after all the years, she was too much a part of him.

Could he stand giving her up, then? No, not that either. Which meant there was no answer to the problem. Except her answer, of course.

It could be a moot point if she was dead. He shook his head, balled his right hand into a fist. He would rather give her up than know that she was dead.

He stood and left the cabin. In the corridor, he was at a loss as to where he thought he was going. Not many choices on a racer. The salon. The bridge. The galley.

The bridge. There might be some activity there. He looked at his watch. Yes, there would be activity. The jump was coming up soon. Nothing to get excited about—just the next step in the frustrating search. Still, a step closer. Remember that. A step closer.

22

❖

The snake was nowhere to be seen, and Iroshi quickly switched the damper off. Although it was late—near midday—it seemed important to have free communication access for a time. One could not know when the right signal would come or be sent that would mean rescue.

She hurried to the stairway, avoiding the elevator access doors as much as possible. Footprints disappearing at the wall would give even Walker and her people an idea of where they were hiding.

She had gotten as little sleep as the intruders down the hill had. It had not taken long to get enough of the crowded elevator car. Much of the night she had spent on top of the car. Before dawn she had climbed the ladder to check the dust on the floor of the rotunda. Even with just the light of the torch, traces of their coming and going were still evident. Walker and company might not see it, but they would be looking for signs even more than she was.

For half an hour she had gathered dust by hand from side rooms and spread it over the floor, backing toward the corridor. It was all right for footprints to show in the center of the rotunda, even in the side rooms. No footprints in the corridor or on the stairs would give them away. Must not be too circumspect, however. In fact, the more in those areas the better, since multiple impressions would only add to the confusion.

As she made her way to the third floor, she and Ensi had debated the wisdom of turning off the damper. The discussion continued while she checked footprints there, too. They had agreed it would be dangerous to send any transmissions, but turning the damper off would also allow the enemy free communications.

"We've already left the damper on all morning," she said. "Varying the times might make them suspect that the damper was not turned off at all."

Unless they are sending continuous transmissions like Captain Ferguson was.

"There's a chance of that. How disoriented are they after last night's entertainment?"

Ensi actually chuckled.

None of them got more than an hour's sleep. I had forgotten how superstitious soldiers can sometimes be.

"When you've killed a lot of people, ghosts seem only natural." She consciously pushed aside memories of a few sleepless nights of her own. "Once they reach the university, we'll have to use the same tactic. At least enough to confuse them. Anything to keep them away from that elevator shaft."

Maybe letting the damper down for the afternoon will be all right. They will be busy searching for us and, once they reach the university, Savron and I will make it an interesting few hours.

She closed the panel and smoothed the dust a little on

that end of the wall, then went back to the door on the first floor. With Ensi's help she checked on the enemies down the hill. Except "down the hill" had gotten closer.

They will be here before nightfall.

"Within the next two or three hours, I would say," she corrected. "We better let Jarys and Mark know."

Ensi's attention went elsewhere, and she waited. Whatever he was listening to or observing might be important. Within a few minutes he returned.

Erik has returned to his body.

"Is that wise?"

It was not a good idea for him to stay in revay much longer. Walker left only three of her people in the camp. He will feign death until an opportunity presents itself.

"What does he plan to do?"

He would like to come back here, of course. His brother's safety and yours are uppermost in his mind.

"Maybe he could take out the people left watching the base of the hill. Tell him to be careful, and under no circumstance is he to return to the racer."

Ensi faded again but returned more quickly than before.

He understands. And he knows of his brother's improved health.

That should cheer him up.

"Now we have to make sure it stays that way. Let's get back to the elevator."

She went up to the second floor, slipping on a step near the top in her haste. After catching her breath, she eased into the access opening. When the time came later in the afternoon to turn the damper back on, she would use the third-floor access. The rest of the time, the second floor seemed the better route since it was darker than the other two and there was less to draw attention.

A quick rap on the hatch brought a muffled response from Jarys. A moment later, Iroshi had joined the medic and Mark.

"Here," Jarys said, holding out a flexible wire with strips of cloth tied at one end.

"What's this for?" Iroshi asked.

"To brush away footprints in the dust. It should work better than using that shirt." She pointed at the dusty garment.

"Thanks." She flicked the sweeper several times. "It just might at that." She sat down on the empty stool. "Our visitors are getting closer. They should be in the building in another two hours or so. From now on, we'll have to be very quiet."

The two looked at each other with veiled expressions. The confinement was already telling on them. She should have allowed them time outside, but she had taken all the work on herself. She *knew* she was claustrophobic. Hardly an excuse for selfishness.

"Jarys, if you would like to take a short walkabout . . ."

The medic's expression brightened, and she nodded.

"Climb to the second floor. I'll follow and show you how to open the access panel." Jarys grabbed hold of the rope rigged to the opening in the ceiling of the car. "Be on your toes. Those people want to kill us. If they find you, chances are they'll get to us, too."

Jarys nodded understanding, a serious expression overlaying her jubilation; then she started up the rope, hand over hand. Iroshi followed while Ensi silently berated her for taking chances.

"We've no way of telling how long we'll have to stay in this hole," she answered him. "This is a chance we just have to take."

Because you feel guilty about not letting her or Mark have some free time?

"Partly," she said, then refused to discuss the matter further.

Once on top, she said down to Mark, "We'll see how close they are. If it looks like they won't get up here as soon as I thought, maybe we can get you out for a while."

"I'm all right," he said, but it was a poor effort at reassuring her.

When she and Jarys returned, she hoped that he really was all right. The enemy had closed the gap in a hurry. Ensi had reported that Walker planned to head for the university before the methodical search brought her there. With that news, it was time to cut Jarys's walkabout short. The medic did not argue in spite of the look of disappointment that turned down the corners of her mouth and wrinkled the space between her eyebrows. If they were lucky—very lucky—the confinement would not last much longer.

Having seen Jarys back to the elevator, Iroshi sat on top of the car and debated whether to turn the damper on right then. However, there were three more hours of daylight. Ensi thought waiting would be all right.

They will probably set up camp before dark some-where down the hill. Walker wants that done before she actually climbs up here. She feels that there is a better chance of catching you if they are all outside and alert, so she will not bring them all with her, but she is growing impatient with their slow pace.

"That's kind of silly, isn't it? I mean, if she sets guards out like she did before, they should see anyone trying to slip down the hill. An even better chance than last night, since the guards will be closer together."

That is assuming that no more ghosts will appear during the night so they can concentrate on their jobs.

"Yeah. Well . . ."

I took a few minutes to check Ferguson. They have left the racer but have kept it in sight. Neither they nor the ship have been discovered. However, he took it on himself to set up one of the beacons on continuous broadcast.

"That will get too much attention."

He set it well away from them. At a great distance, as a matter of fact. I think letting it broadcast for as long as possible will be to our benefit.

"Have you sensed something?"

Not exactly. It might be . . . For a moment, I thought I detected Mitchell. If it was him, he was still quite far away. It is difficult to find anyone when you have no idea where they are in space and time.

"I understand that. But, if you sensed his presence, that has to mean that he's coming this way."

Maybe. Do not let this get your hopes up. Except to leave the damper off for a while longer.

"Of course. We'll leave it off and take our chances on getting it turned on in time."

Mitchell was coming. She had known he would. The thought was reassuring even while it raised the problem of how to . . . The word "handle" had almost come to mind. That was not what she wanted to do, or how she wanted to consider the problem. The most important thing was not to hurt Yail's feelings. Any more than might be necessary. Keeping Mitchell by her side was too important. It always had been important. Sometimes, a strong reminder was a good thing.

The building had been quiet for almost an hour. Darkness in the elevator shaft was unbroken even by her torch as Iroshi silently climbed the ladder. Not even a little light glowing through a crack around one of the doors could be chanced.

Walker and a few of her cronies had already paid a short visit. They were extremely noisy, as if they hoped to scare their quarry from hiding with decibels. The loudest contingent had been three or four men trying to open the elevator door on the first floor so they could look into the shaft. They had found it impossible to get hold of the door edge. They were sending for a pry bar and would try again tomorrow.

Because of their presence so close, it was later than she had intended when she started for the damper. She would have to hurry. The carnivores would start hunting soon. Their transmissions were too overpowering to wait any longer. Anyway, Walker and the others had left the building to finish setting up camp down the hill a short distance, just as Ensi had predicted.

A flash of motion, and her foot slipped on a rung.

Later than she had thought. The beasts were on the move. Hurry, or it would be more than difficult to climb up the rest of the ladder.

Walker is returning.

What else was going to happen?

More movement. Trees flashing past. Her hand groped for the next rung. Two scenes overlaying each other. Confusing.

The leader pulled up. It, too, was confused. The rest of the pack milled around her, whining. Something that had always been there, but different now. They sniffed the air and the ground. The leader placed one paw beyond the old barrier. Another paw. A full step.

The third floor was two rungs closer. Hands were slippery with sweat. Wipe them one at a time down the hip. Move upward.

The ground smelled of the new animal that kept leaving scent. She and her companions had observed the strange creatures at a distance the last two nights. They did not react even when she got close enough to spook most prey. Their scent trail led up the hill.

Hurry, Iroshi. Walker is entering the building.

Panic edged his voice.

Too much input. Everything veiled by everything else. Hard to tell what was real. She reached for a rung, missed, and her feet slipped. For a long moment she hung by one hand, kicking and pawing at the ladder until, at last, she was firmly set on it again.

The access door appeared among the images. She pushed it open. For a moment images from the carnivores faded. Ensi was trying to gain more control, but even he was weakening.

Get to the damper. The door slammed open, and she entered the third floor. She set the lamp on the floor near the wall and turned toward the center of the space, only to stop short. Between her and the machine sat the snake, looking her way, as if expecting her arrival.

Iroshi drew the sword from the sheath at her back. Carefully she checked to make sure the little sweeper Jarys had made was still tucked in her belt. The snake swayed from side to side, hissed, its breath nearly suffocating. Step to the side. It turned. The machine was not on. Why was the creature here, and why would it protect the machine now? And why were the images coming and going in her head?

The snake lunged. One slash across its upper jaw, meant to warn and not cause any real harm. It cried out in pain and surprise and slid backward two feet. Blood dripped darkly in the gloom, mixing with dust on the floor.

She started up the hill, sniffing the trail and the air. The pack followed, excitement raising their hackles. This was new ground for them, new prey. Their excitement came in waves. Both bodies—carnivore and human—quivered.

The tip of the sword wavered. The snake saw or sensed her vulnerability and started toward her. It would die after all. A wave of regret washed through her, and the hunter paused in its climb toward the campsite.

It had sensed her! Transmission might work both ways. That she could transmit had never occurred to her or Ensi. *He* had tried to get through, to influence the animal's behavior, but without any effect. Iroshi was not telepathic herself, only a sensitive. With other humans. How could this new knowledge help?

The snake hissed again. No time to consider new possibilities.

Still determined not to kill it, she rushed forward, slapped its teeth with the flat of the sword, and skipped to one side. Again, the thing howled, then shook its giant head. Before that movement ceased, she rushed in again, hit it between the eyes, danced away.

Its howls shook the walls and filled the air with fetid odors. She could get around it now. Once the damper was turned on, she could fight her way back to the access door. Maybe the snake would run away like it did before.

Walker heard it howling. She is coming up the stairs.

Damn! No time to finesse the thing standing between her and the damper.

"How many this time?"

Two with her. Three staying downstairs.

She started to the right, tripped on something, nearly fell to her knees. The carnivores had the humans in sight. Both entrances to the fallen-down building were covered. Their hearts beat faster, and they slavered. Legs tensed for the spring. The snake moved behind. Light blinded her.

Walker, Ensi gasped.

She waited one, two heartbeats. Seeing nothing except white. Still, she knew when the pack leader leapt. The cries of surprise, human, frightened, angry. Iroshi dropped, rolled in the general direction of the damper. Get it between her and the light.

Too late! A sharp pain stabbed her in the side. The snake? No, not her side. The animal's. It doubled her over.

"Iroshi, you don't know me . . ."

"Your name is Rhea Walker," Iroshi said between gritted teeth.

"My husband was Duncan Walker," Walker said, a trace of disappointment in her voice. "You killed him."

"I . . . never . . . met the man."

One of them slips to the left.

Concentrate on the hardness of the machine against the back. The buttons, knobs, pressing into her. Push everything else aside.

"You didn't have to meet him to ruin him and his business. But I had to meet you before I killed you."

The voice sounded closer, but the sound of footsteps was drowned out by cries and screams inside her head. Human and animal. They were wounding and hurting and . . .

The switch. Must turn the damper on. The left side. Getting her knees under her, Iroshi crept to that side of the cabinet. Get the thing turned on before Walker got any closer. The panel was so much a part of the cabinet and so hard to find.

"That little machine won't hide you forever," Walker taunted. "I saw that thing you were fighting. Looked like it hurt you pretty good."

Walker thought the snake had brought her to her knees.

There. The metal panel popped open. Shaking fingers felt for the switch, slid it in the opposite direction. Images faded, sounds of dying stopped. But still there, on the edges of the mind. The animals hunted within the city walls, so that the damper did not block it all.

Walker yelled, words blurred. A man's voice, shouting, then screaming.

Iroshi shifted the sword from her right hand to her left and stepped clear of the damper. Caught in Walker's torch beam, the snake swayed twice and hissed. A man struggled in the creature's jaws. Walker raised the pistol.

"NOOOOO."

Iroshi rushed forward. No time to draw her own pistol. Only a few steps. Walker fired. The bullet hit the snake between the eyes and it screamed. Blood spurted on its killer, on the floor. The human form dropped to the floor. Warm drops splashed onto Iroshi's face and hands.

The sword swung across, catching Walker in the side, slicing upward into her breast. A human scream rent the air. Walker turned, still gripping the pistol. Fire and thunder exploded from the muzzle. A burning pain sliced across Iroshi's right thigh, and her leg gave way. Both women fell.

The torch rolled across the floor. Concentrate on the rattle and the twisting beam of light. Get up. Knees first. Feet. Sword still in hand.

Walker had managed to turn onto her back, eyes staring up into darkness, glazed over from shock and loss of blood. The gun was out of reach, but Iroshi kicked it farther away. The second mercenary was nowhere in sight. Did he hide in shadow, waiting?

No, he fled when the snake struck.

The snake still breathed, too, but its wounds were also mortal. Iroshi sat down beside its massive head.

It could still harm you, Ensi warned.

She stroked its dry, rough skin, tears blurring her vision, too tired to form a reply. Why did she care that the thing was dying?

Everything deserved to be mourned when it came to the end of its existence.

Even Walker?

"Not by me."

The snake quivered, then lay perfectly still. In the end, it had died so quietly, in spite of its size, its rows of teeth, its bad breath. She gave it one last pat and stood up.

The right leg almost refused to cooperate as she started toward the stairs. Walker had managed to roll over on her stomach, and she crawled ever so slowly toward the gun. Iroshi went over and picked up the weapon, then looked at the sword in one hand and the pistol in the other. Without another glance at her would-be killer, she made her way down the stairs.

Iroshi . . .

"I'll send Jarys up. If Walker is still alive, she can take care of her. If she wants to."

23

❖

Night darkness was broken down the hill by numerous lamps set up in the campsite. Iroshi stood in the doorway of the university, reluctant to move beyond its shelter. Her leg throbbed, giving thoughts a focus other than the silence that waited outside.

Jarys had insisted on tending her leg before checking on Walker. The medic was good, with firm but gentle hands. Mark finished tying up the three mercenaries. He and Jarys had caught them by surprise, having left the elevator against her strict instructions to stay put. While Mark watched Jarys take care of her leg, angry words had risen in her throat; but how could she say them? Mark was a warrior, just as she was. The guilt mounting in his own mind that his leader had been hurt while he was powerless to help was relieved to an extent by the action he had taken. He had failed in his main responsibility. Success of any kind went a long way toward relieving that sense of failure. Ensi and Garon had not needed to work to lessen his sense of failure; the capture of the mercenaries had whittled the guilt down to a duller and smaller stick.

Jarys was not gone long.

285

"She's dead. I couldn't have saved her if I'd gotten there immediately after . . ."

Was she going to say, "After you sliced her up"? No regrets welled up over killing Walker. Sympathy for the snake, yes. It had not deserved to die. And, surprisingly, sympathy for the carnivores. Overwhelming sympathy, and she did not even know if they were dead or if they had run away once the damper was turned back on. There had been a moment, when the snake was dying, when fear and death had seemed to surround her.

The immense snake had been breathing its last, almost lying beside Walker, also dying. Their dying alone could not acocunt for the strength of the feelings.

I believe they are all dead, Ensi said softly, pulling her out of the reverie.

"Yes," she said, finding the strength to head for the campsite.

The building had been a large one, big enough to accommodate all fifteen that Walker had left behind. They lay everywhere, their bodies distorted, their blood dark and thick on the dirt that hid the floor. Animals and humans, their bodies and limbs intertwined in final battle. Eyes stared as if the sight were too ghastly even for them, yet they could not look away.

A whimper from behind made her whirl around, hand on sword. She fought the urge to draw the weapon. In the far corner eyes stared at her, reddened in reflected light, seeing her, fearful, full of pain. Pain that touched her own body, joining that from her leg.

They were too close for the damper to kill death and

fear. The pain flowed from mind to mind, too in tune to block what passed between them.

An impression that the animal was trying to speak, to rise above her own death for something far more important. Iroshi moved to kneel beside the animal that had been an enemy of a different kind. Its body was nearly cut in two. She reached out. The two sections were too far apart. Maybe they could be pushed together. Another whimper rose. Pain, fear of more pain, flashed through her. Pull back. Too close. Feelings too intense. She wrapped her arms over her stomach, trying to hold it all back. Like the snake, the female carnivore was dying, its death slow, the pain a type of death itself. Quivering fingertips reached out, stroked the top of the head. Its fur was soft. The eyes closed a moment.

Iroshi drew her pistol, felt the weight of it in her hand, put the muzzle against the head, behind the ear and pulled the trigger. The head jerked, then fell back, and its eyes, too, stared at nothing.

All of them dead. Two species came together and killed each other to the last one.

She went to the crumbled doorway, stepped into the street, stumbled over a stone. A figure limped from the shadows and blocked her way.

"It's me," a familiar voice said. "Iroshi, are you all right?"

"Yes, Erik. I'm fine. Welcome back."

The sky was still very dark, but daylight was only an hour or two away. He took hold of her arm. She started to jerk away. She did not need anyone's help in getting up the damn hill! Dammit. DAMMIT!

She stumbled again, and Erik's hold on her arm tightened. He led the way to the university and, when they got inside the rotunda, she watched as the two brothers greeted each other. Two survivors. For that she could be glad.

Mitchell ducked as a bullet ricocheted off the tree. Splinters scattered, one striking his cheek. He winced, but only his body registered the hit. His mind was too busy calculating the next move.

When he, Yail, and several Glaive members had landed less than an hour ago, they had found Ferguson and crew under siege. By first count there were twelve mercenaries firing out of the woods. By last count there were only nine left. They had found themselves caught in a crossfire with Ferguson in front and Mitchell behind.

"Yo, the Glaive," a woman's voice shouted. "This is Graham. We give up."

Not surprising, but the surrender did come a little sooner than he had expected. Mercenaries were not always loyal, but they were usually determined. Future employment depended on that kind of reputation.

"Show yourselves," Mitchell shouted back. "There should be at least nine of you able to stand. We see any less, and we start shooting."

Grayson, a member of the Glaive from one of the other racers, nodded, confirming the count.

Figures appeared from behind trees and bushes, arms raised over their heads. Mitchell moved toward the only clear space and, keeping to cover, ordered, "Move toward my voice. Into the clearing."

All but one did as they were told. The ninth man appeared confused about the direction until he finally spotted the others moving away. He joined them. Some Glaive warriors moved through the trees looking for what turned out to be three dead. Of the living, walking mercenaries, two had fairly severe wounds and three slight wounds.

Ferguson appeared and greeted Mitchell warmly.

"I had a feeling you wouldn't be too long in getting here," the captain said.

They grinned at each other. Talking of feelings was an old joke between the two nonmenbers. After they shook hands they watched while the prisoners were searched and their weapons were stacked up.

"We caught the signal after we entered this system," Mitchell said. "Good thing you kept it going."

"What about their ship?" Ferguson asked.

"It won't try anything. It might be bigger than a racer, but it isn't going to take on three of them."

Yail came to stand before the two older men. He looked from one to the other.

"Where is she?" he finally asked, unable to wait any longer.

"In a ruined city about six miles west," Ferguson said.

"Well," Yail began. "Everything is secure here. Let's go get her."

His head jerked around so that he looked Mitchell full in the face. He had been so careful the whole trip, trying not to give away his feelings for Iroshi. His concern had clearly gotten the best of him.

"The comm is clear," Garrick reported. The executive officer had stayed close to the equipment after the fighting stopped.

"Let's see if we can raise anyone," Ferguson said.

As Garrick led the way into the damaged racer, Ferguson described the events of the previous day. After placing the emergency transmitter several hundred yards to the north the evening before, the captain had started everyone into the woods for a better hiding place. Unfortunately, the mercenaries had appeared before they got very far. Retreating back to the racer, they were trapped there until Mitchell and Yail had shown up with the Glaive members.

Garrick sat down at the comm station and began calling Iroshi and Jarys. The others surrounded him, concentrating on the sounds from the speakers.

"Garrick, this is Iroshi," the answer finally came back. "Is everyone all right there?"

She spoke slowly, her voice weighted with concern and something else.

"She's been hurt," Yail said, fear in his own voice.

"Shhh," Ferguson said.

"We are fine," Garrick said. "Mitchell arrived just in time with three racers and crews. Are the four of you okay?"

"Yes. We're fine."

Yail clenched and unclenched his fists.

Mitchell signaled he wanted to talk to her and Garrick gave him the seat.

"This is Mitchell. We'll be there shortly to get you and the others."

"Thanks. We'll look for you."

Mitchell and Ferguson exchanged glances.

"What?" Yail asked impatiently.

"She said she's fine," Mitchell said. "There's something wrong."

"Yes. Someone else or something else." Ferguson nodded agreement. "Let's get there, then we'll find out what happened."

24

✦

"Come in," Iroshi said.

The door opened, and Yail entered her cabin. This meeting filled her with dread. The last thing she wanted to do was hurt the young man. The next to last thing she wanted to do was give him up.

He closed the door behind him and sat in the chair opposite her.

"How's your leg?" he asked.

"Stiff and sore but no real damage."

He nodded. This was going to be harder than she had thought. Might as well just jump in and say what needed saying.

"Yail, I let myself fall in love with you back in Galicia. I should not have done that. It wasn't fair to you." He held his gaze on her so that the hurt stabbed out at her. "I will not give Mitchell up, and neither of us really feels comfortable with the kind of open relationship that would include you. Or any other third person."

He left the chair to kneel in front of her.

"I would not ask you to do that," he said earnestly. "I knew . . . I know that our affair was only temporary. Yes, it hurts, and I will miss you for a very long time. But once I'm back in Galicia, back among familiar places and people, I'll cope. I never expected or hoped that you would give up anything for me."

"Thank you."

She held out both hands, and he took them in his own. Their eyes locked on each other, drawn by pain, and love reflected in each pair. After a moment he rose and returned to his chair.

"Do you want to go back to Galicia?" she asked.

He smiled slightly.

"I had hoped to join the Glaive," he said and pushed the errant strand of hair off his forehead. "But you probably guessed that. Galicia is my home. I suppose I belong there."

"Would you feel better if you could get an appointment as a constable? It could be arranged; you have all the necessary qualifications and experience."

A look of surprise crossed his face, replaced by a thoughtful one. He studied his hand resting on the right arm of the chair for a moment.

"Maybe," he said at last. "Let me think about it."

"Talk to Mitchell. He was a constable when we first met. He could tell you what it's like. The moving from place to place; frontier worlds; that sort of thing."

"Thanks. I will."

A whimper rose from the far corner of the cabin.

"How are they doing?" he asked, pointing at the large, improvised cage sitting there.

"Good so far. We'll need to work further on their diet once we get back to Rune-Nevas."

She stood and went to the cage. The female pup came to the bars, pushing its muzzle through to be scratched.

The male kept its distance, still not quite sure if this large, very white thing was friend or foe.

"They're certainly ugly. Are you going to keep them?"

Yail had come up behind her and was staring down at the miniature carnivores.

"Once they're grown, we hope to return them to their own world. We can telepathically give them the hunting experience to replace their mother's training. They deserve their chance."

"I guess we all do," he said. "I'd better go, see if I can find Mitchell and have that little talk."

She stood and walked with him to the door. He turned to say goodbye, but she put her hand on his cheek. He leaned down, and she kissed him lightly on the lips.

"I do love you," she said.

"I know."

She thought tears glistened in his eyes but could not be sure because of the tears in her own. He turned abruptly and left the cabin. The sense of loss settled even more deeply in the bottom of her stomach.

Did it never end?

Only if you lock yourself away, Ensi said.

That night she slid into bed beside Mitchell, and reached up to brush a stray lock of hair back from his forehead. Grey had softened the brown there and on the sides.

"I'm sorry if I hurt you," she said.

"I know," he said.

"I don't want to live without you. Ever."

He rolled over to face her and touched the tip of her nose with his index finger.

"Me neither. But forever is a long time."

"That's very profound," she said and laughed.

He smiled.

"Yes. I just wish I knew what it meant."

He put an arm around her and pulled her close. It was good to feel safe. Mitchell in her physical world. Ensi filling the empty places of her mind. How many men did a woman need, after all?